THE DEVIL RETURNS . . .

Eloise forced herself to stand tall. A gentleman passing raised a quizzing glass for a better look at her. She smiled radiantly and was rewarded to see the fellow actually stumble. Yes, she still had power over the gentlemen. It was her newfound honor that kept her from using it to the full as she once had. Surely Lord Nathaniel saw her as a lady.

She took a deep breath and turned to see what might be keeping him, but there, moving inexorably toward her, was her phantom. Her stomach jumped into her throat, but she stood her ground, willing him to vanish along with her other fears. He strode to her side but did not bother to bow again.

"Good evening, Miss Watkin," Jareth said. She could only stare stupidly as he took her hand in his very solid grip and brought it to his lips. The warmth of his breath touched her through the silk of her long gloves. The pressure of his lips sent her stomach crashing back down again.

He was real.

He was back in London.

He knew everything about her and had once shown himself black enough that he just might share it.

Faced with such dire circumstances, Eloise did the only thing a lady could do. She let her eyes roll back in her head and collapsed on the floor in a faint.

Other works by Regina Scott

The Unflappable Miss Fairchild

The Twelve Days of Christmas

"Sweeter Than Candy" in
A Match for Mother

The Bluestocking on His Knee

"A Place by the Fire" in
Mistletoe Kittens

Catch of the Season

A Dangerous Dalliance

The Marquis' Kiss

"The June Bride Conspiracy" in
His Blushing Bride

The Incomparable Miss Compton

The Irredeemable Miss Renfield

Lord Borin's Secret Love

And coming in June 2003,
My Heart's Desire

UTTERLY
DEVOTED

Regina Scott

ZEBRA BOOKS
Kensington Publishing Corp.
http://www.kensingtonbooks.com

ZEBRA BOOKS are published by

Kensington Publishing Corp.
850 Third Avenue
New York, NY 10022

All Kensington titles, imprints and distributed lines are available at special quantity discounts for bulk purchases for sales promotion, premiums, fund-raising, educational or institutional use.

Special book excerpts or customized printings can also be created to fit specific needs. For details, write or phone the office of the Kensington Special Sales Manager: Kensington Publishing Corp., 850 Third Avenue, New York, NY 10022. Attn. Special Sales Department. Phone: 1-800-221-2647.

Zebra and the Z logo Reg. U.S. Pat. & TM Off.

First Printing: August 2002
10 9 8 7 6 5 4 3 2 1

Printed in the United States of America

*To Ellen Johnson, for her unflagging devotion,
and to Kristen Skold, for being a woman of character*

One

The most scintillating topic of conversation at Almack's that spring night was Jareth Darby's reformation, and he knew it. As he strolled about London's famous ladies' club for the first time in three years, the air was tainted with the breath of gossip. He could even catch snatches of it.

"Is that not . . . ?"

"It cannot be. Was he not . . . ?"

". . . banished to Italy when he was caught . . ."

". . . and nearly shot in Lady Hendricks's boudoir, but now he . . ."

". . . is tame as a kitten, and that . . ."

"I cannot credit."

Jareth made a point of inclining his head in acknowledgment of the lady's doubt. The round-faced matron went as red as her carmine gown and her equally round companion blanched whiter than the ostrich plumes in her tightly wound curls. Only a beckoning nod from his brother's wife nearby kept him from confirming their suspicions.

"You promised to behave," Eleanor murmured as he joined her and his older brother Justinian.

She stood near one of the statues that dotted the walls at Almack's and it was a question as to which looked more elegant, his honey-haired sister-in-law with her well-molded gown of pistachio silk or the marble bust of Diana beside her.

"I am behaving," Jareth replied, then raised his quizzing glass to appreciate a particularly buxom young lady who was sauntering past.

"On the contrary," Eleanor said, turning violet eyes on him with a look of amusement. "You seem intent on reminding everyone of your reputation."

"I fear he has precious little chance of doing otherwise here," his brother put in, standing straight and tall in his impeccable evening black. "Lady Cecilia Hendricks's disappearance from London still inspires sonnets."

Jareth snorted. "Do you poets have so little inspiration?"

"I could not say," Justinian replied with a wink. "I am a novelist, not a poet. And I remember that you were one of the few to encourage me to show my talents. Now if I can just get you to show less of yours, you may yet hope for a happy life."

Less of my talents? Jareth glanced about the room again. He knew very well which of his talents his brother wanted him to forego. Yet beauty, grace, and temptation were everywhere he looked. Tantalizing perfumes wafted past his nose. Infectious laughter tickled his ears. As he knew to his sorrow, it took remarkably little effort to get the ladies to smile at him, little more to get them into his bed.

But his brother was right that tonight, he must think of only one lady. His future, his best chance at happiness, lay in the hands of Miss Eloise Watkin. For her, he had exerted every effort to be charm itself tonight. He had brushed the blue velvet coat and trousers until their worn nature was neatly disguised. The color had been chosen to highlight the blue of his eyes. His cravat was elegantly tied, his shirt points starched. His wavy pale gold hair was pomaded in place, and he knew from experience that it glowed in the candlelight. Surely a smile, the meeting of gazes, a few tender sentiments and Miss Watkin would melt. He would not leave tonight until she was convinced that he was utterly devoted.

If only she didn't laugh him out of the room.

He'd been dreading the meeting ever since his brother had made his surprising offer. Even now, he could not quite believe Justinian had been so forgiving. The scene in the tavern on the Dover wharf where his brother had granted his request for an audience was deeply etched in his mind. The darkly paneled walls, smells of cheap ale, and cloying cloud of smoke had seemed part and parcel of the life he had been forced to live of late. Justinian, dressed in somber black as he was now, had looked the part of avenging angel.

Jareth had expected to grovel. After the embarrassment with Lady Hendricks, his brother hadn't questioned his decision to remove himself to Italy. Surely Jareth could only expect a frostier reception now that he wanted to return home.

But Justinian had mellowed. Whereas Jareth remembered him mostly as the stuffy, slightly scrawny, and certainly shy scholar, now he stood regally. His thick blond hair showed streaks of gray, but that only made him look more distinguished. Instead of censuring Jareth, his brother greeted him as if he were the prodigal son, clasping his hand warmly and giving him dinner in the private parlor while Justinian listened to his plans to repair his life.

"And it pleases you to work as a secretary to a Member of Parliament?" his brother had asked when Jareth finished explaining himself.

Jareth spread his hands. "It is honest work and a great deal more palatable than hiring myself out as a laborer."

"Then your inheritance is spent?"

"Every cent." Jareth met his brother's thoughtful gray gaze. "Italy is an expensive place, and until recently, my tastes were all too easy to indulge."

"And now you've changed?"

Jareth willed himself not to flinch. He had to appear certain, even if doubts plagued him. If he could not convince Justinian, he would not convince anyone. "Completely reformed," he promised. "I want only to regain some semblance of respect. Will you help me find a position?"

Justinian eyed him. "I think not."

Jareth's chest tightened. This first decent meal in weeks proved to him that he must win his brother over. It was reformation or starvation. Without Justinian's support, he could hardly approach a member of Society for work. He squared his shoulders to fight.

Before he could protest, his brother held up his hand. "Hear me out, Jareth. I knew you would tire one day of the life of the bon vivant. However, I cannot see you so humbled as to play lackey. You may charm the ladies, but you have ever been too vocal in your opinions where the gentlemen are concerned. At times I suspect Lord Hendricks attacked you not so much because you flirted with his wife as the fact that you took him to task over his treatment of her."

"When a man treats his carriage horse better than his wife," Jareth countered, "someone should call him on it."

"Very true, but I suspect the sentiment would carry greater weight from someone other than a renowned rake."

Jareth shook his head. "This is neither here nor there. The fact of the matter is that I have nothing. I must find gainful employment."

"Are you amenable to another suggestion?"

"Certainly, so long as it does not involve charity."

Justinian regarded him wryly. "So, your lusts have changed, but not your pride."

"Once a Darby, always a Darby," Jareth quipped. "You seem the only one not beset with the family vice of puffing ourselves up."

His brother smiled. "It was my wife Norrie who cured me. You shall learn one day, when you meet the right woman."

Jareth had merely returned his smile. Of the dozens of women he'd wooed, only one had ever piqued his pride, and he had never given her the opportunity to do so again.

"I know better than to offer you outright charity," Justinian continued. "I have something else in mind. What do you remember of Cheddar Cliffs?"

Jareth cocked his head. "Adam's personal retreat overlooking Cheddar Gorge?"

"Just so. It was Father's gift to his firstborn son."

"I remember. Alex and I used to say that it was small compensation for having to play the earl. Still if Father's strings were not attached, the estate would have been princely."

"Indeed. Unfortunately, since Adam died four years ago, I have had little time for it. He left a sizeable bequest to see the place well run, but the estate manager is getting on in years and begging for a replacement. Would you like the position?"

Jareth grinned. Could it be this easy? He would not be able to participate in the London social scene year round, as he would have preferred, but Somerset was close enough to justify a week or two every few months. And with money provided for the upkeep of the estate, he could well live the life he loved. "Would I? How soon shall I arrive?"

His brother held up his hand again. "Not so fast. There are still a few strings attached."

Jareth's smile faded. He should have known such an offer would carry a price. "What would you have me do?"

"Nothing onerous. I would simply like proof that your infamous past is over."

"Shall I swear on my life's blood?" Jareth asked. "Present witnesses to my transformation? Fall upon my knees?"

"A combination of the three, I suspect." His brother had the audacity to grin. "Norrie and I are agreed that the best way to set this scandal behind us is for you to gain forgiveness from the ladies you have wronged."

Jareth shrugged. "Child's play. I have never wronged a lady so there is nothing to forgive."

"I believe Society may see it otherwise. Miss Harding, for instance, still laments your loss."

"Two waltzes and a moonlit stroll should not be construed as a declaration."

"And what of the trouble with Lady Charlotte Lenington?"

"She fell from her horse while riding to hounds. I simply took her to the nearest establishment for assistance."

"Yet you cannot blame Lord Lenington for being miffed that his daughter spent the evening in the village tavern playing pennyloo with every worker there."

"Why should he be miffed? She won nearly every hand. Cleaned me out, in fact. I guarantee her father's standing increased among the local population."

"Did you also enhance the reputation of Miss Eloise Watkin?"

Jareth froze. "What do you know about Miss Watkin?"

His brother was watching him. "Very little, actually. Her name appeared among Adam's papers, of all things. Norrie thought you might have known her in Somerset."

Oh, he'd known her all right. He would never forget her. The humiliation of having to work for his supper was nothing compared to the humiliation he had suffered in front of her. Why couldn't his brother insist that he apologize to the young contessa in Italy or the fiery-haired opera singer in Naples? Why couldn't he court forgiveness from some willing widow at a London ball or country house party? He could have more easily found Queen Caroline a pardon than face Eloise Watkin again.

"Adam must have been mistaken," he told Justinian, reasoning that their oldest brother could not have known much about the affair or he would have insisted that Jareth marry the girl. At the time, he might have been willing, for she had been something to like. But remembering the way they had parted ended any thought of reconciliation.

His brother refused to accept that. "Norrie is adamant, I fear. And as Miss Watkin is in London now, she made the list Norrie and I compiled. A dozen ladies in all. Gain forgiveness from each of them, and Cheddar Cliffs is yours."

Except for the inclusion of Miss Watkin, the task had sounded easy. Indeed, in the last fortnight he had smiled, sighed, bowed, and begged to the point that eleven of the twelve had granted him forgiveness. Tonight, he put his skills to the test and faced Eloise.

Though he had been successful in avoiding her thus far, he could not avoid hearing about her as he had moved through London Society. She was rumored to be quite a beauty, which did not surprise him. Her beauty had first attracted him five years ago.

She was also rumored to have distinguished herself in her first Season as a bit of a flirt. Again, that came as no surprise. She had always given as good as she got, and all with a wide-eyed look of innocence. The only thing that had surprised him was that she had reached her third Season without marrying. London gentlemen must have lost their senses since his sudden exit from Society. In his many conquests before and since, he had yet to find a woman to equal Eloise.

They had met when she was attending the Barnsley School for Young Ladies, an endowed school situated on his family's estate near Wenwood. At first he had thought she was a young teacher, which had made her fair game in his book for a liaison. Only later had he discovered that she was far younger and far more ineligible to be the mistress of a rapscallion younger son.

Had things progressed beyond that first burst of lust, he might well have come to a different end. Only when they had been discovered in the hayloft of the school's stables had he been forced to walk away, by a student wielding a pitchfork, of all things. It was the most ignoble moment of his life.

He shook himself and attempted to focus on the present, allowing his gaze to roam the room. He had to gain Eloise's forgiveness, and quickly. He had bartered the last of his jewelry, all but the signet ring his father had given him, for a month's rent in a room in a corner of St. James, and that time would soon be up. Justinian had offered him a place at Darby House, the family townhouse in London, but Jareth had fobbed him off with an excuse of needing his freedom. If he did not succeed in gaining Miss Watkin's forgiveness, he might well be forced to live on his brother's charity, and that thought was untenable. A Darby might fight, whore, or starve himself to death, but he would do so on his own terms.

But surely he needn't worry about Miss Watkin. He had been the one wounded by their affair.

Discreet inquiries made to the school had proven to him that she'd been clever enough to hide their involvement. She had walked away unscathed. Surely she would not refuse to release him from any appearance of wrong doing. None of the other women had refused.

"There she is." Eleanor nodded toward the ballroom floor as Jareth felt his shoulders tense. "Miss Watkin just finished making her bows to Lady Jersey," she continued. "Look, there's Lord Nathaniel leading her onto the floor. You should be able to catch her when she completes the set."

Jareth gazed in the direction she indicated. At least twenty couples stood in the line, but he saw Eloise easily. He caught his breath.

Her midnight hair was swept back from her oval face to fall in ringlets down her back. The high-waisted gown of emerald silk revealed the alabaster of her shoulders and neck and draped the curves of her body in graceful folds. He did not have to be closer to know that her eyes were a vivid shade of green, intriguingly slanted, and masked by lustrous black lashes. He could remember those eyes all too well—alight with pleasure, deep with passion.

He was more afraid of what those eyes would show now. Would he see anything but contempt once he mustered his courage and asked her pardon?

Two

Eloise Watkin smiled at Lord Peter Nathaniel as she passed the young viscount shoulder to shoulder in the dance. By the look of admiration in his soft brown eyes, she had him. Perhaps Cleo was right: he would offer marriage before the week was out.

"Smitten," her friend the young marchioness had proclaimed only yesterday when they had returned from a fortnight's house party at the Nathaniel family estate outside London. "He danced attendance on you every moment. Everyone remarked on it."

Eloise could not argue there. She knew when she was the object of gossip; tongues had wagged far too often about her for her to ignore it. However, she had to own that it was novel to find the gossip pleasant in nature.

It was also rather satisfying. She had worked hard the last year to shed the bitterness and fear that had once plagued her. She had determined to be a woman of character. It was rewarding to find that London Society seemed to like that woman as much as she did. While she wasn't willing to concede that Lord Nathaniel was utterly devoted to her, she was willing to agree that he appeared quite taken. A shame that the fact did not thrill her as much as it did Cleo.

Lord Nathaniel squeezed her hand as she took his for a promenade, and she chided herself on her attitude. Any young lady should be pleased to attract his regard. He was gentle, thoughtful, and endlessly polite. He was also wealthy, titled, and possessed of a good family. His short brown hair curled endearingly around a cherubic face. His physique was manly, if a bit on the heavy side. He always dressed with restraint. No one, she was sure, would find fault with his camel-colored coat of wool superfine or buff pantaloons. Even his white silk cravat was simply tied.

She was pleased he had sought her out. His family was known for having exacting standards when it came to the qualifications of brides. Indeed, she had never quaked quite so much as when she had been presented to his mother last week. But Lady Nathaniel had been as gracious as her son. Surely the fact that they accepted her was proof that she had finally achieved respect among the members of the *ton*.

Cleo was just as certain. "You are making your mark at last," she had told her earlier as they waited for Cleo's husband, the Marquis of Hastings, to escort them to Almack's. "I cannot tell you how delighted I am that you have put that reprehensible Jareth Darby out of your mind."

Eloise had merely smiled. Truth be told, if Cleo knew how often she thought of Jareth Darby, her friend would surely despair.

It was difficult to forget the first man she had ever loved, even more so because he had forsaken that love. His attentions had seemed so romantic then. Even now, there were moments she found Viscount Nathaniel sadly lacking in comparison. Of course, the chivalrous viscount was also far less likely to trample her heart. She should apply herself to the task of cementing her place in his affections.

She followed him through the pattern of the dance, fluttering her lashes from long practice and casting him covert glances from the corner of her eyes when they passed. With an odd number of couples in the line, she knew that she and Lord Nathaniel would have to take a turn standing out. When they stepped aside, she smiled brightly at him.

"I so enjoy our time together, my lord," she confided, gazing at him from under her lashes.

His smile was warm. "As do I, Miss Watkin. And may I say that you dance divinely?"

She kept her smile to herself as she made a circle with the toe of her green kid slipper on the polished wood floor, knowing the movement drew attention to her long legs. "You are too kind, my lord."

"Not at all." His assurance was fervent. "Rarely have I seen anyone so poised. Many young ladies show an inappropriate passion for the dance." He nodded down the set to where Lady Thomas DeGuis was laughing as her doting husband swung her to the left.

Eloise felt a slight chill and wished for the paisley shawl she had brought with her. She forced herself not to be so common as to rub her arms where they were bare between her long gloves and the cap sleeves of her satin gown.

"You cannot compare my feeble skills to those

of Lady DeGuis," she told the viscount. "Besides, surely passion such as hers should be praised."

"Yes, I had heard that her efforts for the unfortunate here in London are tireless," he allowed, eyeing the lady in question thoughtfully before returning his gaze to Eloise. "As are yours, I believe. Did I not hear that you are assisting her?"

Eloise smiled. "For the last few weeks. I find her work admirable and was lucky that we shared a mutual acquaintance in Lord Hastings. I prevailed upon him to introduce us. He is a great admirer of the lady as well."

"Some ladies should be admired," he murmured, taking her hand for a quick kiss. Eloise willed the caress to thrill her, but instead the only emotion she felt was a minor satisfaction. She took his hands to return to the dance.

But though she danced with her usual flair, she found herself repeating his words in her mind. He admired her. Lord Hastings admired her. Lady DeGuis admired her. It appeared that the entire *ton* thought her worthy of admiration.

How would they react if they knew the truth?

The thought was completely unwelcome. She brought her foot down so firmly that Lord Nathaniel raised his brows. He could not know why she had to deal with such thoughts as firmly as she'd stamped her foot. She would not be ruled by fear any more than she'd once allowed herself to be ruled by passion.

She knew the consequences of the choice she'd made all those years ago. Though a married woman might carry on any number of affairs if she were discreet, an unmarried woman of London Society could not admit to an indiscretion without forfeiting her future. That was why her romance with Jareth Darby remained a closely guarded secret.

As far as she knew, only four people other than herself knew of her past. Cleo was her dear friend and would have died rather than breathe the secret to a soul. Her husband had become a friend and ally as well; Eloise knew she could count on Leslie to remain silent. Miss Martingale, headmistress of the Barnsley School for Young Ladies, had already proven she wanted no one to know that one of her charges had been less than chaste. That left only the villain of the story, Jareth Darby, and he was safely in exile on the Continent.

Determined to capture the future she desired, she smiled and flirted and danced with ladylike restraint for the remainder of the set. Her performance must have been particularly convincing, for, as soon as the dance ended, Lord Nathaniel implored her to join him on a stroll about the hall. She glanced across the room to where Cleo was engaged in conversation with her husband and several others. Her friend would not miss her. She accepted his offered arm and they set off.

Along the edges of the dance floor were any number of sofas and alcoves where people gathered to converse. The first group they passed contained Lady Jersey, their hostess for the evening. The queen of London Society nodded in greeting as they passed. Eloise smiled in satisfaction.

"Particularly lovely weather for this time of year," Lord Nathaniel commented politely.

"Oh, decidedly," she said with more enthusiasm than the tired subject warranted. They passed a group of dowagers who smiled at them with approval. Eloise raised her head.

They passed another group, this one of young people who talked and laughed, animated, carefree. One of the young men raised a lady's hand to his lips in tribute and she gazed at him raptly. Eloise swallowed.

Suddenly a laugh turned to a shriek, and one of the ladies darted away from the group, directly into Eloise's path. She recognized Portia Sinclair, who was on her first Season.

Lord Nathaniel stopped with a frown, but Portia seemed heedless of his presence. Her attention was all for the young, dark-haired Major Churchill in dress regimentals, who had followed her from the group. She tossed her red-gold hair and swung a quizzing glass from her short fingers, daring him to retrieve it. When he reached for it, she slid it deftly down the tight bodice of her white muslin gown, then laughed at the look of chagrin on his handsome face.

"A sorry showing," Lord Nathaniel murmured as he detoured around her. "I believe Miss Sinclair grows more shocking with each ball."

Eloise glanced back and saw that Portia and the major were in deep conversation. Indeed, it was as if they had forgotten anyone else was in the room. She had been just as besotted. She shook her head. "Surely her activities can be ascribed to nothing more than high spirits."

"You are being kind, Miss Watkin. You see only the good in people."

Would that it were so, she thought. In truth, it was all too easy for her to suspect the worst of everyone she met. "I am merely speaking from my own experience," she assured the viscount. "I was much like her, once."

"Never say so," he replied, pressing her hand on his arm. "I will not believe you were ever anything but perfect, Miss Watkin."

"You are too kind, my lord," she returned, but somehow his praise did not warm her.

They passed two more groups before Lord Nathaniel spoke again. "Will you be receiving callers later this week, Miss Watkin?"

She blinked, but quickly recovered her poise. Was this what she had waited for? "Certainly, Lord Nathaniel," she assured him. "I hope I shall always be home to you."

"Now, you are too kind," he murmured. He paused, and she was forced to stop as well. He gazed warmly down at her. "I hope you know, Miss Watkin, that I hold you in the highest esteem."

His voice positively trembled with emotion, and Eloise could not help but be touched. He truly was a worthy fellow. "I hope you know, my lord," she replied, "that I highly esteem you as well."

His look grew even warmer, and she thought that if they had not been in Almack's, he might have kissed her. She felt a momentary flutter at the thought. He did not seem to notice, merely squeezing her hand with fervor before turning her back the way they had come.

"I should return you to your friends," he said.

She was ready to agree when she saw him.

Along the wall in the direction they were moving stood Jareth Darby, staring at her. The man and woman at his side were staring as well, but Eloise barely noticed them. She could not take her eyes from Jareth. He looked much as she still pictured him, tall, lean, confident, platinum-haired, and devilishly handsome. She could not seem to take in more. Indeed, all coherent thought had fled. She must have hesitated, for Lord Nathaniel's grip on her arm tightened as if in support.

"Is something wrong, Miss Watkin?" he asked.

She shook her head, more to clear the apparition than to answer him. The dance ended, and couples parted. People passed her, intent on securing new partners. When she could see down the wall again, the tall, elegant woman stood alone. The devil had fled with her composure.

She let out her breath. Was this some dream of her feverish brain? He could not be in London. Surely she would have heard. No, more likely her thoughts of matrimony had conjured him. It was a sign of her uncertainty in the future, nothing more. All perspective brides were allowed second thoughts.

"I am fine," she assured Lord Nathaniel. "Perhaps just a bit winded from the dance."

"Quite understandable. Shall I procure you a glass of lemonade?"

The thought of being alone was suddenly terrifying. She glanced about, but saw no sign of Cleo or Leslie. She clutched at his arm. "No, that is unnecessary. If we could find a seat?"

"Of course." He paused to glance around the room. "Ah, yes, I see a free sofa directly opposite."

She followed his gaze and gasped. Standing beside the sofa, resplendent in his coat and breeches of blue velvet, was Jareth Darby. He must have noticed her staring, for he made her a bow.

"Do you see him?" she asked, voice barely above a whisper.

"See whom?" Lord Nathaniel asked.

The crowds milled and parted again. The space beside the sofa was empty.

A laugh bubbled out of her, sounding hysterical to her. "Apparently no one. Perhaps I need that lemonade after all. My mouth is suddenly quite dry."

"Your servant, madam." He bowed over her hand and strode across the floor, to be quickly swallowed up in the crowd going toward the refreshments.

Alone, she wrapped one arm about her waist. What was wrong with her that she conjured ghosts? Did some part of her not believe she deserved a kind, considerate husband like Lord Nathaniel? She thought she had stamped out those fears and self-doubts. She had earned her place in Society. She had prayed, reformed, done good deeds to atone. She had been accepted. She refused to lose that acceptance now and by her own imagination.

She forced herself to drop her hold and stand tall. A gentleman passing raised a quizzing glass for a better look at her. She smiled radiantly and was rewarded to see the fellow actually stumble. Yes, she still had power over the gentlemen. It was her newfound honor that kept her from using it to the full as she once had. Surely Lord Nathaniel saw her as a lady.

She took a deep breath and turned to see what might be keeping him. Moving inexorably toward her was her phantom. Her stomach jumped into her throat, but she stood her ground, willing him to vanish along with her other fears. He strode to her side but did not bother to bow again.

"Good evening, Miss Watkin," he said. She could only stare stupidly as he took her hand in his very solid grip and brought it to his lips. The warmth of his breath touched her through the silk of her long gloves. The pressure of his lips sent her stomach crashing back down again.

He was real.

He was back in London.

He knew everything about her and had once shown himself black enough that he just might share it.

Faced with such dire circumstances, she did the only thing a lady could do. She let her eyes roll back in her head and collapsed toward the floor in a faint.

Three

Jareth caught her neatly, but not before cries of alarm arose on all sides. He quickly found himself the center of attention. He had hardly expected a welcome from Eloise, but he somehow hadn't thought she'd be the one to faint from the encounter. He could think of nothing he had done to warrant such a reaction. Still, it was difficult to look innocent standing in the middle of Almack's with a beautiful woman in his arms. By the expressions of the ladies around him, he was swiftly being painted the villain. He offered them his most winning smile as he shifted his grip on Eloise.

"Heat fatigue," he assured them all. He loosened one hand to pat her cheek. "Miss Watkin, are you all right?"

He hadn't expected a response and was surprised when her lips moved.

"Go away."

He blinked and peered closer. Thick curling black lashes fanned out over alabaster cheeks. The only other spot of color was her soft, rose-toned lips. She always had been the most kissable female. That hadn't changed. But now was hardly the time to find out if she still tasted as good as she looked.

"Miss Watkin?" he tried again.

She sighed and opened her eyes. Green as deep as a forest in summer nearly took his breath away. "Let go of me," she said firmly.

Jareth did so, and she wobbled to her feet. The ladies around them began talking all at once. The sound was no doubt supposed to be soothing, but Eloise turned so pale that he put a hand on her elbow to support her. She stiffened at his touch.

"What happened?" someone cried, and Jareth looked up in time to see a pint-sized Amazon push her way through the crowd, with a tall, dark-haired man at her heels. She had reddish-brown hair set in short curls around a pert face and her well-molded bosom heaved with righteous virtue. She didn't fool him for a second. The last time he'd seen her, she'd had a pitchfork in her hand and she hadn't been afraid to use it. She seemed to have the same idea now.

"You!" she declared, evidently recognizing him as well. It was all he could do to hold his ground. "Release her this instant," she demanded.

He would have been delighted to do so, but Eloise disengaged from him first. "Mr. Darby has no hold on me, Lady Hastings," she said calmly.

"Nor should he," the Amazon maintained hotly.

The tall gentleman, whom he took to be the Amazon's husband, God have mercy on his soul, stepped forward and put a hand on his wife's arm. "Perhaps we should continue this conversation in private, dearest."

She looked ready to protest, but evidently

thought better of it. Perhaps it was the pointed look Eloise gave her. He could have kissed her for that. None of them needed another story circulating. Of course, he seemed to think of kissing in connection with Eloise far too easily.

They started to move away, and he knew he had to act quickly or lose his chance. "Forgive my interruption," he tried, stepping to Eloise's side. "I would like a moment of Miss Watkin's time, when she is feeling better, of course."

Eloise refused to meet his gaze. He could do nothing but bow and turn to leave. He found Lady Jersey blocking his way. She stood tall in her amethyst satin gown, her pomaded golden hair glinting in the candlelight. Her impressive bosom wasn't heaving, but the fire in those blue eyes was enough to make him cringe.

"Are you disturbing my hall, Mr. Darby?" she said, though the simple words implied blasphemy worthy of hell fire.

He swept her a bow. "Certainly not, my lady. Miss Watkin evidently collapsed from the heat. I merely managed to cushion her fall."

"A likely tale." The young man who had been dancing so cloddishly with Eloise pushed his way to the front. The fingers of his gloves were stained from the punch that still trickled over the glasses he held in a trembling grip. "I have heard of you, Darby, and nothing good. I demand to know what you did to Miss Watkin."

Jareth raised his glass and glared at the fellow through it. Before he could speak to put the upstart in his place, help came from an unexpected source.

"I am certain Mr. Darby was merely trying to help," Eloise said quietly.

Jareth blinked at her sudden change of heart. Lady Jersey and the young lord frowned.

"If you would excuse us," the Amazon's husband said, "I think Miss Watkin needs to sit down."

The young lord bowed, and Jareth had no choice but to do likewise. He watched as Eloise was led off to a sofa as far away from him as possible. The young lord followed. Deprived of drama, the crowd dispersed. Lady Jersey clucked her tongue.

"Bad *ton*, Mr. Darby. I shall keep an eye on you."

"I can only try to earn your approval, dear lady," Jareth replied with another bow, this time to her.

She raised a brow that said she very much doubted his abilities to please her in any proper manner, then sailed off to join another group. As he walked toward Eleanor and Justinian, he heard the murmurs begin afresh.

"He is unchanged . . ."

"Just as scandalous as always . . ."

"Did you hear how he was forced from Society the last time?"

Jareth grit his teeth. He had only made things worse. Justinian and Eleanor apparently thought so as well, for they hastened to join him as if in support.

"What happened?" his sister-in-law asked, her silk gown whispering almost as loudly as she did.

Jareth shrugged. "I cannot say. The lady simply collapsed."

"Odd," Justinian said. His gray eyes were thoughtful as he gazed to where Eloise had been settled. The Amazon and her husband ministered to her as she accepted her glass of punch at last from her fawning escort. She certainly managed a smile for his sake.

As if she felt Jareth watching her, she glanced up. Their gazes locked. For a heated moment, he was back in the hayloft over the school stables. He could smell her lilac perfume merging with the scent of summer hay, feel the silk of her skin beneath his hands, hear the sweet gasp of her breath as he covered her with kisses. Eloise turned on the sofa to put her back to him.

The cut direct.

Justinian must have seen it as well, for he shook his leonine head. "How disappointing, Jareth. You are obviously far from forgiveness."

"Indeed," Jareth murmured. The fact ought to annoy him but he found himself intrigued. He was the one who had been forced from the hayloft in disgrace. Supposedly, no one knew of the lady's transgression. They had never promised each other undying devotion. What grudge did she bear him?

"Who is that with her?" he asked Eleanor.

She peered across the room. "The young woman beside her is Lady Hastings. Her given name is Cleopatra, if memory serves. The handsome fellow with the jet black hair is her husband, Leslie Petersborough, Marquis of Hastings. They eloped to Gretna Green last Season."

Still the impetuous one, Jareth thought. "And the boy in brown?"

"Lord Peter Nathaniel," she supplied.

"And he is hardly a boy," Justinian added. "He inherited the title and estates from his father several years ago."

"By the look of things," Eleanor continued, "he has serious intentions toward Miss Watkin."

Which made Lord Nathaniel even more of an upstart than Jareth had originally thought. He could not see Eloise with a fellow whose hands trembled. He could not imagine the man having the courage to make love to her. On the other hand, he could imagine himself doing so all too easily.

Before he could comment further, someone bumped him from behind. Turning, he found a slender girl with red-blond hair righting herself with a rueful smile. "Pardon me, please," she said, giving him a glimpse of front teeth with an endearing gap between them.

He swept her a bow. "My mistake entirely, I assure you."

Her smile deepened, and he caught a decided twinkle in her gray eyes. "Nonsense, sir. I distinctly remember bumping into you."

He could feel Eleanor and Justinian watching him. Further, over the girl's shoulder, he could see a tall major in dress regimentals glowering at him. It seemed the better part of valor to send her on her way.

He bowed reflexively. As she hurried away, he sighed. Another time he might have been willing to investigate the delightful young lady's charms, but his hands were tied until he had dealt with Eloise. It would be impossible to convince her he had changed if he was known to be pursuing another woman.

"That was boldly done," Eleanor commented as he turned toward them once again. "Have you been introduced to Miss Sinclair?"

"No," he replied. "Shocking what they teach young ladies these days."

Justinian chuckled, but Eleanor shook her head. All of them returned their gazes to the unwilling Miss Watkin. Eloise sat on the sofa for a short while, then left on the arm of Lady Hastings. They did not return to the hall.

Deprived of his reason to visit Almack's, Jareth took his leave of Eleanor and Justinian, as well as Lady Jersey, and collected his cane and cloak. Then he descended the stairs for the street to hail a hack and repair to the civilized confines of White's.

He had favored Watier's in his earlier days, because that gentleman's club was known for its heavy play and high stakes. Very likely, the more conservative White's would never have allowed him membership but for his brother's intervention. As it was, he was welcomed, offered a drink, and motioned to a comfortable chair. He did not realize that he had been followed until he wandered into the card room. Before he could decide whether to attempt Faro with only credit, he was accosted.

"Darby, I demand a word with you."

He turned to find Eloise's escort beside him. Lord Nathaniel appeared to have run all the way from Almack's, as his curly brown hair was wild and his white silk cravat in disarray. Jareth merely eyed him coolly.

"I am not in the habit of giving my time to fellows who refuse introductions," he said, purposely turning away from the young lord. The gentlemen playing nearby raised brows or exchanged glances. One went so far as to chuckle. The rudesby at his elbow stalked around to face him again.

Jareth gave him no time for speech. He turned away again and strolled over to settle himself in a chair near the bow window. Unfortunately, he had no sooner eyed the gas light beyond the window when Lord Nathaniel was once more in front of him and considerably redder.

"You will not evade me so easily," he declared. "What I have to say requires no introductions. You, sir, are no gentleman and I take offense that you expect to be treated like one."

"You can take as much offense as you like," Jareth told him, crossing one leg over the other, "so long as you take yourself off."

"Not until you hear me out. You are unwelcome, sir. Your reputation precedes you. I demand that you refrain from tainting others with it."

Jareth deliberately sipped his drink before answering. "If you dislike being tainted, why accost me in public?"

Nathaniel drew himself up. "*My* reputation is unassailable, sir. My concern is for a certain young lady."

"Then I take it her reputation is less than savory."

He wondered whether a fellow that young could die from apoplexy. His face certainly was a shade of red seldom found outside a house of ill repute.

"Not at all," he sputtered. "And I intend to see

that it stays that way. I do not know what you said to Miss Watkin at Almack's, but she is so overset that Lady Hastings had to take her home immediately. Tongues will wag, sir."

"Yours certainly does," Jareth replied. "Since when is it appropriate to mention a lady's name in this place? I should call you out for your impertinence, sir."

It amazed him to see how quickly the crimson fled, leaving Nathaniel's round face pale as blanc mange. But to do the fellow justice, he stood his ground. "I should be happy to have my seconds call on yours, sir."

Jareth waved his free hand. "I have no interest in adding to my reputation with your sorry death. Allow me to assure you that you need not concern yourself. It is clear to me that I have offended the lady. I will not approach her again in public until she has forgiven me."

His opponent had the audacity to smile, and a rather nasty grin it was on one so otherwise boyish. "Then my quest is accomplished. You will never approach her, Darby, for she will never forgive you."

Jareth returned the smile with one of his own, and, he thought, one not much more pleasant. "Oh, but she will, my dear sir, if I have to spend every moment of my existence assuring her that I am utterly devoted."

Four

"I am doomed," Eloise told Cleo as they rode home in the Hastings's coach.

"Surely it isn't that bad," Cleo replied, but even in the dim light of the coach interior, Eloise saw her husband's hand grip Cleo's. More realistic than his wife, and more experienced, Leslie had to know what she was facing. Indeed, his dark thoughts were evidenced by the tight lines of his handsome face.

"Explain things to her, my lord," Eloise said.

She saw him squeeze Cleo's hand. "Sorry to burst your bubble of optimism, love, but Miss Watkin is correct. I doubt she shall have many offers if the truth becomes known."

Even though she knew the gravity of the situation in her heart, hearing him say it sent a chill through her. She'd had five years to think about what she'd do if she met Jareth Darby again, five years to calculate to the last frown the amount of damage her liaison with him could do her. Even her friendship with the Marquis and Marchioness of Hastings could not save her.

"What truth?" Cleo demanded, clearly unwilling to be swayed. "The fact that she was nearly a child when he took advantage of her? The fact that she has led an otherwise exemplary life?"

Eloise grimaced. "Hardly exemplary. Indeed, if you had not taken me to task last year for my behavior toward others, I could very well have alienated all of London."

"But you didn't," Cleo protested. "And no matter what happens, your friends will stand by you."

"And who are my friends besides you and Leslie? I began driving others away long before I met Mr. Darby. You are a dear for forgiving me the times I doubted you. I have not been so fortunate elsewhere."

"Well, you cannot blame the other girls for shying away from you when we were at school. Few people deal well with perfection."

Eloise sighed. "You must believe me, Cleo, it was never my intent to snub anyone. It was your honesty that helped me see how I was not acting like the woman I wished to be."

"However, Cleo is right," Leslie put in. "Your behavior of late has been remarked upon, and kindly."

"She is much changed," Cleo added with evident pride. "Even Lord Owens confided that he had misjudged you, and I know you remember how he ceased his suit for you last year. He knows you are a different person now."

Eloise could see Leslie smiling as he gave his wife's hand another squeeze. "I would argue that Eloise isn't so much changed, my dear, as she has finally decided to hoist her true colors." He nodded to Eloise. "And I sincerely hope that you do not let Jareth Darby force you to fly a false flag again. You have too much to offer."

His words and Cleo's support eased her heart, yet she could not seem to stop the churning of her mind. The last year of her life had been the best since she was a child, largely because of her friendship with the Hastings. Just tonight she had been sure she had achieved her goal of being a woman worthy of acceptance, appreciation, approval. Why did Jareth Darby have to reappear in her life now!

By the time they reached her father's townhouse on Curzon Street, she had regained some of her composure. She suffered the butler to solemnly remove her cloak.

"His lordship is awaiting you in the garden withdrawing room, Miss Watkin," he intoned.

"Thank you, Bryerton," she replied. Although she'd lived in the house with her father since graduating from the Barnsley School three years ago and knew the various rooms well, she let the butler lead her. His step was slow and stately, as if he ushered her to her coronation rather than a late night conversation with her father. Such was Bryerton's way.

He had served her father for many years while Lord Watkin had been in the diplomatic corps but he did not seem to approve of Eloise. It was as if she were somehow a hindrance to the efficient management of the house. One had only to look at Bryerton's regal bearing, the powdered wig he still affected, and the impeccably tailored black velvet coat he wore to know that he took his position as head of the household staff seriously. If his demeanor were not enough, the spotless glow of the stately rooms with their corniced ceilings, pastel-colored walls, and buffed wood floors would have told her that the household staff marched to strict orders and considered polish next to godliness.

At times, she wished for a less formal existence, but her father seemed to relish it. Now he responded with a curt answer to the butler's rap at the door to the second-floor withdrawing room that overlooked their small garden.

As Eloise entered on Bryerton's heels, she saw that her father was sitting in a scroll-backed chair near the wood-wrapped fireplace, freshly ironed evening paper in front of him. His spare form was clothed in his usual brown suit and tan-striped waistcoat. Like Bryerton, he held to an immutable order of things, which seemed to include never allowing his daughter to see him in less than a formal setting. Tonight she would much rather have curled up beside him on the sofa, but she knew better than to suggest such a thing.

"Miss Watkin to see you, my lord," the butler announced as if she'd been away years instead of a few hours.

Her father put down the paper. A smile lit his thin, pale face. "Ah, Eloise. Come in. Tell me about Almack's."

Eloise hesitated only a moment before going to stand before him. A part of her would have liked nothing better than to throw herself into the seat beside him and tell him exactly what had happened and how much it concerned her. Before retiring from the diplomatic corps, her father had traveled throughout Europe. She'd heard that he'd seen any number of volatile affairs and found ways to smooth them. Surely he'd know how to handle Jareth Darby.

The only problem was, he had no idea what Jareth meant to her.

Besides, Bryerton was stationed beside the door, and she didn't want to speak of sensitive subjects in his hearing. So she remained standing and returned her father's smile. "Almack's was a bit tiring tonight. But I did dance with Lord Nathaniel. He requested to call later in the week."

Her father's pale blue eyes were thoughtful. "Does this please you?"

Even before Jareth had appeared she hadn't been certain of the answer to that question. Now that he threatened her future, she was even less sure. "He's a good man," she said defensively. "Stable. Courtly. He honors me with his interest."

"He should be the one to feel honored," her father told her. "But I look forward to meeting this paragon. Now perhaps you should retire. You look worn."

"I am a bit fatigued," she allowed. She dropped a respectful curtsey. "Good night, Father."

Her father inclined his head, and Bryerton stepped away from the wall to lead her to her bedchamber.

Normally, the pale blues of the bed hangings and draperies in her room were calming and peaceful, but tonight they did not comfort her. Neither did her maid, Martha. The older woman had a round face that was surprisingly stern with narrow-spaced eyes. Her movements were quick and sure. Eloise was never tempted to linger over brushing out her hair at night or bathing in the morning. Everything ran on schedule with Martha.

Still, she thought, as she slipped beneath covers

that Martha had efficiently heated with a warming pan, at least Martha was better than the chaperone she had had the last two years. Miss Tidwell had had endless advice, but Eloise had soon found that the woman had little interest in acting on that advice. Instead, she used any excuse to leave Eloise to her own devices. When Eloise had had a near-scandalous run in with Leslie, before he had married Cleo, Lord Watkin had been convinced to discharge the chaperone and hire a maid instead.

Eloise had hoped that Martha would be someone in whom she could confide, but just as Miss Tidwell had been all talk, Martha was all action. And her actions were as strict as the whale-bone corset with which her considerable bulk was constrained. She did her work with a prim, "yes, Miss," "no, Miss," and disappeared into the nether regions of the house. Once in a rare while, Eloise actually won a smile from her, but it quickly vanished. Like Bryerton, Martha seemed to feel that it was singularly inappropriate to mix with the master and his family.

When Martha left her alone that night, Eloise sighed. She felt unaccountably blue-deviled. It would be all too easy to cry. But she'd shed more tears than she liked over Jareth in the past and a few tears weren't going to change her life today. Better to focus her attentions on how she might achieve her goal of living happily ever after now that Jareth had reappeared.

She knew she would not feel comfortable entering marriage without explaining her past to her prospective husband. However, she certainly didn't want Jareth to be the one to make the explanations. Of course, he might say nothing, but she couldn't take that chance, not when Lord Nathaniel was so close to proposing. Yet how could she ensure Jareth's silence?

He had no conscience, or he would never have abandoned her. His family was wealthy, so he hardly needed money. She could offer him neither position nor connections that could not be bettered by a simple conversation with his brother. The only thing left to bargain with was her virtue, and she refused to give him a chance at that a second time.

The one factor in her favor was that the story of their passion reflected no better on him than it did on her. He'd been the youngest son of a wealthy earl, and terribly spoiled. Even then, few were foolhardy enough to censure him.

She'd been the only child of a couple much in love and just as prone to be spoiled by their attentions. But when her mother had died, her father had become withdrawn. More and more his work took him away and she was left in the care of others—nannies, governesses, chaperones. Still, she tried to please, always eager for praise. She knew the reports to her father glowed with her accomplishments. She could sit her horse by eight. She had mastered the piano at nine. She spoke fluent French and Italian by eleven. Her father should have been delighted, but as she never received more than an occasional letter, she could never be certain.

At fifteen, she had been enrolled at the Barnsley School for Young Ladies. While the teachers were more exacting than her tutors, again she excelled. Within a few months, it was common for the staff to refer to her as the example.

"Stand taller, Miss Pennybaker. See how Miss Watkin glides across the floor."

"More blue in that water color, Miss Courdebas. Notice the fluidity of Miss Watkin's waterfall."

"Relax in the saddle, Miss Rutherford. Look at how Miss Watkin becomes one with her mount."

As Cleo had reminded her that night, her fellow students had either worshipped her or been jealous enough to hate her. Either way, what she did was imitated, what she said, repeated. She was queen of her world and confident in her ability to rule.

So was their headmistress, Miss Martingale. The imposing woman was so pleased with Eloise's performance that Miss Martingale insisted she be allowed to accompany the teachers to their annual tea at the Darby estate. Most of the school staff had been too awed to do more than stammer answers to the questions asked by Helena Darby, then the Countess of Wenworth. Eloise, however, had had no trouble being charmingly polite to the elegant young countess. Lady Wenworth had been immediately won over.

She remembered how content she'd felt as she followed the teachers on a tour of the palatial country house. As they ventured on, she had stood alone for a moment in the Darby family chapel, gazing up at the golden cross, and thinking she could get no closer to heaven than she had today.

She had gotten closer, and had been knocked nigh unto hell because of it.

Even now, she could hear him as she had that

first time. "Bright angel, have you fallen that I a
lowly mortal should find you here?"

The voice, rich and warm, had fit so well with
her mood and thoughts that she had only smiled.
Turning, she'd been amazed to find that she had
not conjured the sound. A man had appeared as
if from her desires.

He was beautiful. His hair was the color of polished platinum and his blue eyes were bright as
crystal. The light through the stained glass window sparkled around him like fairy dust, silhou-
etting his lean body. He had evidently been out
riding, for he wore shiny black boots, skin-tight
chamois trousers, and a tweed riding jacket with
velvet lapels. She wasn't entirely sure what he
thought of finding her in his family chapel, for
surely he was a Darby, but she knew admiration
when she saw it. To see it from him stole her
breath.

"No angel, sir," she'd answered shyly. "Merely
a maid."

"Ah, but what a maid," he chided, striding forward to kneel at her feet. She gazed down at him
in wonder. His upturned face was sweet, implor-
ing, worshipful.

"Dearest maid," he murmured, "grant my wish.
Make me immortal by thy kiss."

Oh, how very tempting he had been. But then,
he'd always known how to tempt. Even that first
day, she had been willing to risk all for him. She
had bent down to touch her lips gently against
the crown of his head. He'd smelled of leather
and sunlight. The silken curl of his hair teased
her cheek.

He'd sighed as if her mere touch brought ecstasy. She could well imagine that, as the kiss had affected her nearly as much. He rose fluidly to his feet and clasped her hand. "I cannot say all I wish here. Meet me tonight, at the lightning-struck oak behind the school stables. Midnight. The wait will seem an eternity."

Before she could protest the impossibility, he'd brought her hand to his lips and pressed a fever-ish kiss into the bare skin of her wrist. His touch undammed a flood of emotions. The only thing that stopped her from acting at that moment was the sound of Miss Martingale's voice calling from the corridor.

"Promise me," he'd begged against her skin.

She'd nodded, retrieved her still-tingling hand, and hurried after her teachers. The rest of the tour she'd hugged her hand to her heart even as she hugged the memory.

Even now, she found the memory potent. He'd been so romantic, so dashing, made up of equal parts of danger and delight. It had taken little to persuade her to throw everything she'd been taught out the window, if only she could be with him. What a shame he had turned out to be some-one who cared for nothing but himself. A greater shame, she supposed, that she'd spent much of the intervening five years bemoaning her choice. No more. She had worked too hard, come too far.

Whatever the cost, she vowed, Jareth Darby would find it much more difficult to persuade her of anything this time.

Five

Jareth lost no time in attempting to see Eloise again. The hesitation he had felt in approaching her vanished in the face of her coolness. She offered him the first challenge he had been given in a long time. With Cheddar Cliffs as the prize, he could not fail to meet that challenge. Determined to make his case, he appeared at her home at the fashionable hour of three in the afternoon.

"I regret to say," her hard-faced butler informed him with nose so high Jareth wondered he didn't drown in the rain, "that Miss Watkin is not at home."

More annoyed than deterred, he tried again the next day and the next, leaving his card each time. He tried calling early and late. He tried returning in a quarter hour in hopes he might catch her coming home. In all cases, the butler refused to allow him admittance.

He kept trying, but by Saturday evening, he had yet to see the lady again. He considered breaking his word to Lord Nathaniel and accosting her in public, but decided against it. She was just as likely to cut him again. He resolved to wait on her front step, if need be, until she returned. Eleanor, who, with Justinian, had joined him at the theatre, pointed out that Eloise would likely not be receiving until Sunday afternoon and he might as well come to church with them in the morning. Neatly cornered, he'd been unable to find an excuse to refuse.

The sermon at St. George's Hanover Square was uninspiring. In fact, it seemed calculated to annoy him, being based on the text of David and Bathsheba. The similarities with his reason for leaving London did not go unnoticed. Of course, David had lusted after Bathsheba and he had merely rescued Lady Hendricks. He did not think it wise to mention that to the good reverend.

As his mind wandered with the sermon, so did his gaze. He noted with amusement who was squirming and who was snoring. Several ladies seemed intent on attracting his attention, even two who had husbands in tow. The mothers of the younger women seemed equally intent on disabusing any notions of his suitability. They at least knew better than to put stock in his attendance at church.

One particular young lady, two rows in front and to the right, continued to glance back at him. The third time he noticed he realized it was the Miss Sinclair who had bumped into him at Almack's. The light from the candles in the nave danced over her red-gold hair and silhouetted her slender form. She should have looked angelic only her glances toward him were anything but. Only the obviously pointed whispers from the woman next to her (he assumed her mother) forced her gaze to remain forward for the last part of the service.

It was only as he rose to leave that he saw that

Eloise had been sitting a few rows behind him. She wore a white muslin gown trimmed with pink rosebuds and satin ribbon. He had no trouble picturing her as an angel. Unfortunately, that only reminded him again of their first meeting. A shame all he could ask of her was her forgiveness. A greater shame that she did not appear to wish to grant even that.

She saw him watching her and leaned to whisper something in the ear of the older man who accompanied her. Surely he must be Baron Watkin, but he looked nothing like his daughter, excepting his translucent skin. Jareth was highly tempted to push past the dowager ahead of him in the pew so that he might reach Eloise, but he forced himself to shuffle slowly toward the aisle. By the time he was free, Eloise had disappeared.

He dashed out of the church, raising no few brows in the process. He didn't have to hear the gossip this time to know its content. By galloping out of the house of heaven he was once more proving he belonged to the house of hell. He did not let the sentiment deter him from scanning the steps and pavement around the chapel. She was nowhere to be seen among the crush of carriages.

But he was undaunted. It was Sunday after all. Surely this would be a day to grant forgiveness, if it were asked. Leaving Justinian and Eleanor to thank the minister for the service (and apologize for Jareth's behavior, if needed), he hailed a hack and went straight to the Watkin townhouse.

"Miss Watkin is expecting me," he told the butler when the solemn fellow answered his knock.

"I regret to say that Miss Watkin has not informed *me* of that fact," the butler replied. "Shall I take your card, sir?"

"As you already have a sizable collection, I think not. However, I should be happy to wait while you request additional guidance from the lady. Just promise her that I come as a penitent."

"One moment, sir."

The butler's idea of a moment clearly differed from Jareth's. He counted off one hundred and fifty moments before the door opened again. By that time, he'd tipped his hat to six ladies, nodded to four gentlemen, and smiled appreciatively at five pieces of prime horseflesh.

"As I expected," the butler said, "Miss Watkin is not at home."

"Then I will wait until she is at home," Jareth informed him.

The butler merely looked at him. "I regret that we seem to have no space available for you to wait, sir."

Jareth flipped back his tails and settled himself on the front step. "Then I shall wait right here," he called back over his shoulder.

The butler didn't even sigh, though Jareth suspected he was hard pressed not to. "The under footman generally sweeps the front step at half past one, sir," he said solemnly, "and it is nearly that now. I am certain you would not want to dirty your trousers."

"I certainly would not," Jareth retorted, glancing down at his dove gray trousers, one of the few of his belongings that didn't need refurbishing. "In fact, if such a thing were to happen, I would likely cry out. Loudly. Repeatedly. I should think your neighbors on the terrace might remark upon it, unless of course they are also not at home."

The door slammed shut.

Jareth waited. He'd never liked having to wait. If he had, there might be fewer ladies on Justinian's list. Certainly Eloise wouldn't have been on it. From the first, he could not get enough of her.

He had never doubted she'd appear at the oak. He'd felt her interest in the chapel. She would come, if only to be sure of him. Having ridden all his life in the Darby woods, which they shared with the school, he knew exactly how close he could come to Barnsley without getting caught. He'd tied his horse at the oak just before midnight and lit a hooded lantern. But he didn't need its feeble light; he could hear the footsteps hurrying toward him.

She burst into the small clearing, cheeks flushed and eyes wide, her slender form enveloped by a rich burgundy cloak fit for royalty. Now he realized the expense of the cloak should have been a clue that she was no impoverished teacher. Then it had seemed fitting raiment for her beauty and their secret meeting. A few leaves clung to her ringlets as if Oberon himself had crowned her. Seeing him, she stopped and sucked in a breath. He was suddenly afraid she'd run back the way she'd come.

He swept her a bow in the glow of the lantern. "Ah, Titania, Queen of the Fairies, well met."

She stood a little taller, but some of the tension seemed to fade from her. She cocked a brow. "This morning I was an angel and now I'm a fairy. Have you seen fit to demote me, sir?"

"Never," he assured her fervently. He laid a

hand on his chest. "Queen of the angels or queen of the fairies, you remain queen of my heart."

Her regal air vanished as her eyes widened again. "Really?"

The surprise vested in that single word should have been another clue, this time of her youth and inexperience. Then, he had been too intent on making her his to question anything she said or did. He had hurried to assure her of his utter devotion.

They had met nearly every night like that for almost a month, sometimes at the tree, sometimes elsewhere in the wood. At first, she had allowed him no more than a few chaste kisses that merely left him hungry for more. Occasionally, he'd consider giving up, but something in the way she'd look at him in parting, green eyes flickering beneath dark lashes, would encourage him to keep returning. That and the way her laughter tickled more than his ears. And the way her smile made him feel taller, more clever, and infinitely more handsome than his older brothers. In fact, she'd made him feel as if he could do no wrong.

Until that fateful night in the stables.

He shook himself. What was he doing reveling in the past when his future was in jeopardy? He and Eloise had chosen to go separate ways. Time to earn her forgiveness and get on with it. Jareth began to whistle.

When nothing happened, he started a hymn. *While Shepherds Watched Their Flocks By Night* gave way to a rousing chorus of *Oh God, Our Help in Ages Past*. It wasn't until he exhausted his meager knowledge of proper songs and moved on to tavern ballads like *The Busty Barmaid of Berkeley* that the door opened again.

"Miss Watkin will see you now," the butler intoned as if nothing untoward had happened.

Jareth rose and followed him into the townhouse.

He had always considered the butler to be too high in the instep to belong to someone as winsome as Eloise, but the interior of her house suited her no better. The colors were pale and lifeless, the furnishings bare of ornamentation. Even the stiff-backed woman in the portrait over the stairs looked uncomfortable. He straightened his cravat self-consciously as the butler led him up the stairs to a withdrawing room at the front of the house.

The room was just as Spartan, with its cool colors and uncushioned wooden chairs, but the sight of Eloise in one of them did much to raise his spirits. However, as he moved closer he could see that she held herself so stiffly her back failed to touch the lyre pattern of the wood behind her. Her hands, sheathed in lace gloves in the pattern of roses, were so tightly clenched in her lap that he thought she might pop a seam. He bowed, and she nodded her permission for him to sit. The butler stationed himself beside the door.

"I apologize for the inconvenience," Jareth said by way of preamble. "But I must speak with you."

"No, you must not," she replied firmly. "We have nothing to say to each other, Mr. Darby. I granted this interview to make sure you understood that."

He spread his hands, offering her his most charming smile. "But Miss Watkin, I am a changed man. I am determined to overcome my past and restore myself to the bosom of my family."

She stared at him. "You have reformed?"

"Completely," he assured her with what he hoped was sufficient fervor. "I seek to gain forgiveness from all those I have wronged."

"All of them?" She raised a brow. "I should think that would take some time, Mr. Darby."

He refused to flinch. "Actually, it has been mercifully quick. The other women whom I have approached have been eager to see me walk the path of righteousness. Indeed, my brother is so convinced of my change of heart that he promised me a position managing one of his estates."

"Indeed."

Her decidedly chilly tone was not the least encouraging, but he pressed on.

"Knowing you as I did, I felt sure your generosity of spirit would shine forth and you would also support me in my change of heart. I realize we parted under difficult circumstances, but I assure you that I bear no ill will."

Her green eyes were as cold as the waters of the North Sea. "How very charitable of you, to be sure."

Her sarcasm was so obvious he knew he was in trouble. He would have to try harder. He went down on one knee before her. Her eyes widened in obvious surprise.

"Miss Watkin, Eloise," he implored, gathering her icy hands into his warmer grip. "Surely you remember what we once meant to each other. I realize you may feel differently now, but could you not find it in your heart to forgive me?"

Her posture seemed to grow even more rigid. She withdrew her hands from his. Her rose lips pulled back over straight white teeth.

"Never," she spat.

Six

Eloise had the pleasure of watching Jareth blink in confusion. It would have been even more satisfying if he had flinched or cried aloud, but, given his black heart, confusion was probably the best she could hope for.

"I beg your pardon?" he tried.

"Yes, you did. You begged my pardon and I refused to give it. Completely understandable given our situation, I should think."

His look lightened, intensifying the blue of his gaze. "Of course. I was too sudden. Forgive me for not explaining myself further. The delight of seeing you again tied my tongue."

So, he still thought words would be enough to sway her. She crossed her arms over her chest. "Your tongue, Mr. Darby, seems to be the only thing that is working, for if your brain were as agile, you would understand why I cannot forgive you."

When she did not elaborate, he frowned, silvery brows lowering over his long nose. "Perhaps my brain is addled, as you say. Please tell me what concerns you."

She could feel Bryerton standing by the door and knew she could not tell Jareth all she had to say. She settled for the most grievous sin. "You did not think to contact me before now?"

"I did not dare," he replied simply, with that smile that would once have made her heart flutter in her chest. The fact that it was nearly doing that very thing now only made her sit straighter.

"You did not dare or you could not be bothered," she accused.

"I assure you it was the former. I thought it best not to make our connection more widely known." He cocked his head, bringing her attention to the way his platinum hair curled around his ear. "I had my valet inquire about you, but when he returned with no bad news, I assumed I was the more affected by the event. After all, I'm the one who ended up with a scar on his . . ."

She bolted to her feet. "That will be all, Bryerton!" Scowling at Jareth for putting her once more in an untenable position, she waved the butler out.

But just as Jareth could not conceive of his own faults, so evidently Bryerton could not conceive that she would purposely break with propriety.

"Shall I escort Mr. Darby to the door, Miss Watkin?" he asked in evident confusion.

"No, thank you," she said pointedly, feeling herself grow redder with each word. "I must speak with Mr. Darby, alone."

Bryerton's facial expression did not change from its usual solemnity, but by the way he stiffened she knew she had offended him. Still, he obviously did not want to compound her error with one of his own, namely to point out how scandalously she was behaving.

"As you wish, Miss Watkin," he intoned. He

bowed himself out, leaving the withdrawing room door conspicuously open.

She shook her head. He was obviously trying to salvage her reputation, even if she would not. But her father was just down the corridor in his study, and she could well imagine that he would walk by or even walk in while she spoke with Jareth. She walked to the door and shut it. Turning, she found Jareth regarding her thoughtfully.

"I take it our former association is a close secret," he said.

"Well, I certainly avoid the topic," she assured him. Squaring her shoulders for battle, she marched back to face him. "And if you are sincere in this tale of reformation, you will not want it shared either."

He immediately brightened. "I am sincere, I assure you. All I ask is your forgiveness."

Was it as easy as that? Could she simply lie, say that all was forgiven, and have him disappear from her life? He would not speak to her father. He would not speak to Lady DeGuis. He would not speak to Lord Nathaniel. She could not believe her good fortune. She opened her mouth to grant his request.

But the words wouldn't come.

Jareth was regarding her, and she managed a feeble smile while her mind whirled. What was wrong with her? *What was wrong with him?* another part of her insisted. Did he truly think a simple apology was all it took to wipe away his past? He claimed to have sent his valet to inquire about her; it seemed a lie at worst, and far too easy at best. He had made her think that he cared, then walked away, leaving her to bear any consequences from their actions. Given that, how could she even consider granting forgiveness so easily?

He was obviously not so much changed that he thought he would have to atone. No, he still thought all he needed was a charming smile and a ready wit. Even now, he smiled at her as if certain she would acquiesce to his request. The injustice was great, but her need for his silence was greater. Too much hung in the balance—her present, her future. She tried to force the words out, but nothing came. Why could she simply not say the words he wanted to hear and send him on his way?

Perhaps it was the look of supreme confidence in those clear blue eyes.

"You never required my forgiveness before," she pointed out. "Why do you want it now?"

She knew she must have grown wiser then because she saw the change in him. He stood just a little straighter in his black coat and dove gray trousers, and his gaze skittered away from her. He didn't want to answer that question. Why?

"I want your forgiveness now," he said, "because it would ease my conscience."

She felt a laugh bubbling. "Now, there's a lie. You, sir, have no conscience."

He shook his head, the sunlight from the window behind them making golden highlights on his thick wavy hair. "Certainly I have a conscience. Perhaps it just uses a different scale of measurement from yours."

"Oh, I am certain that it must. And I am just as certain that it does not motivate you in this instance. What does, I wonder?" She cocked her head and regarded him steadily. He shifted his weight ever so slightly from one foot to the other. She had to hide a grin. This was simply too much fun! The thought that she could actually discompose the infamous Jareth Darby was quite heady.

"Come now, Mr. Darby," she challenged. "Out with it. Why are you really here?"

He shrugged. "Believe me or not, madam. I truly came only for your forgiveness."

She felt a jolt of disappointment and put it down to having her fun thwarted. She tried to get him to answer again. "What, no other motivation? Perhaps I can guess. Is it that you have fallen in love and your new lady requires proof that you are a gentleman?"

He snorted. "Any lady who would accept such feeble proof would not be worthy of my love."

She was willing to accept that, but frowned at the feeling of satisfaction that curled through her. Some part of her appeared delighted that he was not in love, likely the part that wanted to see him suffer.

"Then it must be your family who requires it," she guessed. "Perhaps they will not allow you into their bosom until you prove yourself reformed."

"My brother has been kindness itself," he assured her. "I even accompany him on outings. You saw us in church today."

She certainly had. She hadn't thought devils were allowed on sanctified ground, but there he'd been, acting as pious as the rest of the congregation. She had felt a momentary start when she realized that Lord Nathaniel was sitting but a few rows ahead of him. Her gentle viscount had indeed come calling that week as he had said, but she had been chagrined to find that his conversation was even more stammered than usual. He had been unable to bring himself to offer for her. She could not allow him to converse with Jareth before he was truly hers.

But as upsetting as the idea of losing Lord Nathaniel had been, what had been more upsetting was the way her eyes were drawn to the glow of Jareth's pale hair in the church's lamp light. When he turned his gaze, she had marveled at the clean line of his profile. When he stretched his arm out along the back of the pew, she had remembered how it felt to have that strong arm wrapped about her. Even now, watching him fidget through her questioning, she felt the memories stirring. She shook herself, determined to remain on course.

"If not love or loyalty, then," she said, "money must be involved somehow."

This time there was no mistake that he stiffened. She gasped.

"That's it, isn't it? What, have you made some wager about me this time? Am I merely a line in the betting books at White's?"

His face was hard. "I have told you my motivation, madam. I wish to clear my conscience and return to a normal life. If you think otherwise, you don't know me."

"On that we quite agree," Eloise said, sure she had found the true reason for his behavior and incensed by it. "And I assure you that had I known what you were, I would never have let you near me."

Those eyes were chips of ice. "And what exactly am I?"

"Do you require a listing of your many sins?

Perhaps we could start with the more obvious ones. You are a liar and an adulterer."

He shook his head. "And you, madam, listen far too much to gossip and slander."

She raised her brows. "What, do you pretend innocence?"

"I feel no need to justify myself, to you or anyone else."

"And why not? You came here asking for my forgiveness. If you are such a paragon, for what must I forgive you?"

He sucked in a slow breath, as if trying to maintain his civility. "In truth, I am not sure. Perhaps coming here was a mistake. Apparently, you have made up your mind, and nothing I say can sway you. Therefore the only thing left is to bid you good day, madam." He snapped a bow and started for the door.

Eloise stared after him, suddenly deflated. That was it? After all that, he wasn't willing to fight for the forgiveness he claimed he wanted? No begging? No pleading? Even after all this time, he could not even offer so little as a conversation.

Yet, inexorably, he stopped. She could see his shoulders rise as if he had taken a deep breath. He turned toward her, and she was the one to inhale sharply. Those eyes seemed deeper somehow, sadder. She felt her heart touched and struggled to keep the walls she had erected against him.

"I am a coxcomb, Eloise," he murmured. "I see no reason for you to hate me so, but for the very fact that you do, I should apologize."

"On that," she said quietly, "we can also agree."

He took a step back toward her. "Is there nothing I can do to persuade you that I have changed? Nothing I can do to make amends?"

"Fall off a very high cliff onto some very sharp rocks?" The words were out before she thought better of them.

He shook his head with a wry grin. "Perhaps something less violent? I paid good money for this coat once. Jagged rocks and blood would do it little good."

She could see he was trying to tease away her anger. Would that it were so easy. She had thought she had put this episode of her life behind her, that she had come to terms with the choices she had made. But it was apparent something held her back from closing that door. Surely it was the fact that she had been the only one to bear the consequences.

If only she could show him the damage he caused! If only she could make him understand the humiliation and pain his ladies must feel when he walked away and left them to sweep up the pieces. For once, just once, she wanted Jareth Darby to feel what it was like to be the one with regrets.

Was that possible?

He must have seen some change in her for he stepped forward once again.

"What is it?" he asked almost eagerly. "Have you thought of some way you could forgive me?"

She had, and it was something so perfect that she could not believe she had discovered it. Jareth claimed to have a conscience. If that were true, she had only to get him to use it. She might never erase the hurt she still felt from their parting, but if he realized the damage he had done, he might prevent himself from hurting anyone else.

And if he didn't have a conscience, she need feel no guilt for punishing him the way she planned. Besides, if she planned the punishment appropriately, she might be able to prevent him from telling anyone about their past. Either way, she was free.

"I have an idea," she allowed. "It remains to be seen whether you will be willing to try it."

"As long as it does not involve sharp objects or loaded pistols, I am certain I will approve."

"Very well, then." It was all she could do to refrain from rubbing her hands together with glee. "You claim to have changed, Mr. Darby. I require proof, a challenge, if you will."

He smiled, spreading his hands. "I am yours to command."

"We shall see. I propose three tests. Pass all three, and I shall bestow my forgiveness. Fail even one and you will never approach me again or speak one word about our former association. Is it agreed?"

He eyed her. "Perhaps I should hear about the tests first, given your bloodthirsty predilections."

She faltered. She had hoped to concoct them as she went, using the inspiration of the moment. But he mustn't know that. She straightened. "The exact nature of the tests is immaterial. Besides, if I told you beforehand, it might give you an advantage."

"Heaven forbid." His smile told her he was humoring her. She couldn't wait to see that smile fade.

"But if you insist on keeping it dark," he added, "I must insist on a few caveats to my acceptance."

"Such as?" she asked suspiciously.

His blue eyes glinted in challenge. "No test can be paradoxical. You cannot ask me to retrieve the moon or stop the sun."

She wrinkled her nose. "Children's wishes. I would not be so foolish."

He nodded. "Good. You will also not require me to do anything that could cause me or anyone else bodily harm."

"What do you take me for?" she demanded. "Certainly, I would never ask you to harm another."

He inclined his head in acknowledgment. "Finally, you cannot require me to spend a penny. No fripperies or trinkets from the local jewelers."

"I begin to think I should call this off now," she said coldly, "if you truly think I would use this as an excuse to wrangle a bauble from you."

"You have changed, madam. How am I to know what you are capable of now?"

How indeed? She would show him, and well. She smiled. "As you will. I accept your terms. Are we agreed?"

"Agreed." He offered his hand, and she accepted it. Before she knew what he was about, he brought her hand to his lips and pressed a kiss against her knuckles. Heat licked up her arm. She snatched back her hand.

He grinned as if he knew exactly the effect he had on her. "So, when do we start?" he asked.

"Tomorrow," she replied before she could lose her courage. "Meet me at Berry Brothers and Rudd on St. James at eleven in the morning and you will be given your first test."

Seven

As soon as Jareth left, Eloise called for the carriage. She simply had to tell Cleo what she'd done. She was rather glad her friend received her in the wood-paneled library of the Hastings's townhouse and refused refreshments. Eloise's hands were shaking so hard she was certain she'd never be able to hold a cup of tea.

"I must be mad," she told her friend as they sat on the heavy wooden chairs the library boasted. "But I find myself actually enjoying the thought of tormenting him."

"I think your choice was inspired," Cleo assured her, brown eyes glinting with malice. "We have both heard rumors of the number of ladies he has wronged. Tomorrow you strike a blow not only for yourself but for all of them as well. If only I knew their names, I would issue personal invitations."

Eloise couldn't help but giggle at that. "We might even sell tickets and donate the money to Comfort House."

Cleo clapped her hands. "No, I have one better: we could enter a wager in the betting books at White's on his ability to complete your tests.

The men will be sure to take his side, and we will win a fortune!"

At the mention of the betting books, Eloise sobered. "I would give much to see those books right now. I believe he may be trying to win a wager at my expense."

Cleo scowled. "We shall shortly see about that. I shall ask Leslie to check when next he visits. Just be certain you show Mr. Darby no mercy tomorrow. After what he did to you, he should be thankful you were no more vindictive. Hercules had twelve labors, if I remember correctly."

Eloise shook her head. "I will have a difficult enough time coming up with three, I assure you. And if I cannot keep myself from remembering his more tender moments, I might not even manage three."

"Tender moments?" Cleo's dark eyes widened. "He had tender moments?"

Eloise giggled again. "What, did you think I would be attracted to a monster? I assure you, he has earned his reputation for wit and charm. I doubt few ladies can resist him when he is intent on his game."

"Is that why you—" Cleo stopped herself, reddening so that her skin clashed with the apricot gown she wore. "Forgive me, Eloise. I have no right to ask you that."

Eloise suspected she knew what Cleo wanted to ask. "You are my truest friend, Cleo. If you cannot ask me, who can?"

Cleo hesitated a moment longer, then blurted out, "How could you have given yourself to him? I mean, you were only fifteen, nearly a child. It just isn't done!"

"Oh, I suspect it is done far more often than our teachers would lead us to believe," Eloise told her, though the mild censure stung. "But, the simple fact was that I fancied myself so deeply in love that nothing else mattered. I would have flown to the moon and back had he asked it of me. Anything else seemed trivial."

Cleo smiled, but the look held sadness. "I feel the same way about my Les, but I know the feeling is reciprocated."

Eloise thought her own smile must be just as sad. "I thought the feeling was reciprocated too. But had he loved me, he would never have left." She shook herself. "You see? If I dwell too much on the past, I will never face my future."

Cleo had been encouraging then, but the note she sent Eloise the next morning was even more so. In Cleo's sprawling hand the letter read:

> *Leslie reports that Jareth Darby is mentioned in several wagers, but none that appear to include you. In fact, the only wager being made about you is whether you will accept Lord Nathaniel when he offers. Note that that is when he offers, not if. I shall shortly be wishing you happy, in several areas it seems.*
>
> Your devoted friend,
> Cleo

So, the male members of the *ton* expected Lord Nathaniel to offer for her. The thought was rather pleasing. However, the news that Jareth was not betting on her forgiveness was simply confusing. She had been so sure by his reaction that money was at the heart of his quest. If not a wager, then what?

She was no closer to an answer when she spotted him in the crowd strolling St. James. He had stopped to speak with Portia Sinclair and her stepmother. His conversation made them both simper. Portia's color was nearly as bright as the pink ribbon on her serpentine spencer. Her slender hands kept fluttering over the drape of her green-sprigged muslin gown as if uncertain how attractive she looked.

On the other hand, her stepmother's dark gown should have made her look as stern as Eloise, who was dressed in navy lustring. Yet even Mrs. Sinclair appeared to be captivated by Jareth's charm. Her small mouth was bent in a smile; her pudgy cheeks were rosy. He was supposed to be reformed, yet there he stood for all the *ton* to see, making ladies' hearts go flutter.

Her blood heating, she managed an equally insipid smile as he broke off his conversation with a bow and strolled to meet her just as distant church bells rang a quarter past eleven.

"You are late, Mr. Darby," she informed him.

He reached for the pocket of his embroidered waistcoat as if to retrieve a watch, then seemed to think better of it. He bowed instead.

"I was unavoidably detained."

"So I saw," she replied, gaze drawn past him to where Portia and her stepmother were watching. The older woman must have noticed Eloise's pointed look, for she tugged on Portia's arm, turning her away.

"Do you know Miss Sinclair?" he asked as if making polite conversation.

"Yes. An interesting young lady, to be sure, as are all the other young ladies making their debuts. Do you intend to discuss their merits as well, or shall we get on with this?"

He raised a brow. "Are we in such a hurry then? Is there some urgency to this test of yours?"

"No," she had to admit. "But I do have other activities planned for the day, so if you wouldn't mind?"

He bowed again. "I am at your disposal."

She felt her mouth curl in a satisfied smile. "Excellent. The first test, Mr. Darby, is of your humility. I was certain that must be one area in which you sought to reform."

"Indeed; I am far more humble than when you first knew me."

It was a pretty speech, but he spoiled it by pausing to flick a piece of dust off the lapel of his navy jacket.

"Indeed," she said.

He glanced up, obviously noting the sarcasm in her tone. "You think that impossible? Test me as you will, madam."

"Oh, I shall, Mr. Darby, I shall." She turned to nod down St. James toward White's. Even this early in the morning, gentlemen would be lounging by the windows. He would be easily noticed. "You see the bow window at White's? I intend to walk from here to there. I expect you to follow behind me."

He quirked a smile. "My angel, you are kindness itself."

"On your knees."

He blinked. "I beg your pardon?"

"You did indeed, and if you complete this feat,

you will be on your way toward earning it. Your test, Mr. Darby, is to follow me the length of St. James on your knees, as befits a true penitent."

He glanced up the street as if measuring the distance. She followed his gaze, noting the number of people. Ladies walked arm in arm, followed by footmen loaded with packages. Gentlemen strolled by, swinging canes of ebony and teak. Street vendors hawked wares, their cries rising over the sound of passing carriages and wagons. Urchins darted through the crowd in search of fun and a fat purse. Jareth's eyes narrowed.

"I believe we agreed that I would not be required to do anything dangerous to my health."

"Your physical well being, certainly. But you appear to be in fine shape, Mr. Darby. Surely a little stroll such as this is not too difficult for you."

She was certain he would not argue the point and she was right. Instead, he found another problem.

"But if I follow you in such a manner, will not people remark upon it? How will you answer without revealing our past?"

Although she had already considered the matter, she felt herself blushing. "If we are questioned, we will simply say that you offended me at Almack's and seek now to assure me of your utter devotion. You are utterly devoted, are you not?"

"I am your abject servant," he gritted out, though his gaze continued to assess the street before them.

"Then I am certain this test will not present a problem for you," she replied with a smile. "Will you try my test or are you willing to admit that you are not so changed after all?"

He turned his gaze on her then, and she felt the heat of it. "I have changed, Eloise. If this is what you need to prove it to you, then I accept."

She should have been disappointed that he did not give up right away, but instead she felt an absurd sense of pleasure. "Very well, then. Down you go."

He knelt on the pavement. His light-blue trousers strained against the muscles of his legs and outlined his powerful thighs. Flustered that she had noticed, Eloise whirled and started off down St. James. Immediately he called out.

"Not so fast, blast it! You never said this was a race."

She slowed, biting back a smile. If he wanted to prolong his torture, who was she to argue?

She schooled her steps to a saunter and opened her lace-edged blue parasol to shield her from the sun. To her immense satisfaction, people began to stare. She did not have to glance back at him to know he was there. The looks of those passing assured her that he was a sight. When the crowd and carriages thinned momentarily, she even heard the shuffle of his boots as he dragged them along.

"You had better pick up your knees, Mr. Darby," she called back. "Your valet will have apoplexy if you ruin the shine of your boots."

"I have no valet," he informed her testily.

"Just as well," she replied, giving her parasol a twirl, "as I expect the knees of your trousers will not survive either. I would not want to give the poor man reason to leave you when you return home in rags."

His response was a disgusted grunt.

They continued down the street. Some people grinned when they saw her shadow. Others raised a brow or scowled in censure at such a display. Eloise kept her head up. Well did she remember similar looks on the faces of her schoolmates when she had been brought to the headmistress' office.

Cleo had felt compelled to confess what she had seen in the hayloft. Now Eloise knew her friend had been trying to help, but then she had only felt betrayed yet again. Cleo thought Miss Martingale would understand Eloise's predicament, perhaps even insist that Jareth Darby do right by her. Eloise would never forget the headmistress' words.

"I am very disappointed in you, Miss Watkin. I expected better."

She felt her smile slipping now at the memory and forced it back into place. She had survived the humiliation that was the consequence of her choice. Now it was Jareth's turn.

And humiliation it was. Ladies of quality crossed the street to avoid being seen near him. Gentlemen refused to meet his gaze. The street vendors pointed and laughed. Some went so far as to stop traffic for her as they crossed King Street. A daring urchin threw a half-eaten apple. Eloise did not turn to look at Jareth, but she knew he must be mortified.

Yet as they continued down St. James, she began to notice different expressions on those they met. Ladies' faces puckered. Gentlemen looked thoughtful. Street vendors sobered, and urchins sighed. She could not imagine what they saw in him until she heard Jareth's voice.

"Alms! Alms for the poor!"

She whirled, nearly colliding with him. He had his top hat in one hand and already it rattled with coins. Somewhere along the route he had found charcoal or soot, for he'd smeared it across his forehead and cheeks until he looked like a chimney sweep. His coat was dusty, his shirt tail hung out in damp folds, and he'd gone through one knee of his trousers to show cool skin wearing raw. When she gasped in surprise, he grinned, and she realized he had been sucking in his lips to appear toothless as well.

"Give a poor bloke a shilling for vittles, milady?" he whined, holding out his hat.

She pushed it away. "Stop that at once!"

"Now, now, Miss," scolded an older gentleman just passing. "We must be patient with those less fortunate." He dropped a penny in Jareth's hat and continued on.

"God bless yer, guv," Jareth called after him.

"You are impossible," Eloise declared. "You have failed, sir. Take yourself off this minute."

"On the contrary," he replied. "I intend to continue the length of the street. Press on, my dear."

"I refuse to have you following me like this!"

He shook his head. "You must. You promised: no paradoxes. I cannot follow you down the street if you refuse to lead."

She glared at him. Around her, people continued about their lives, dropping coins in Jareth's hat, casting her curious glances. Now she was the object of scorn. She could not allow him to get the best of her. She faced forward, resolute.

"Unclean!" she cried. "Clear the street! Typhus!"

People paled, cried out, and scuttled away from them as fast as they could. She waved her hands and set off at a sharp pace. "Typhus! Yellow fever! Make way!"

Behind her she heard Jareth curse as he tried to keep up.

By the time she reached White's, she was nearly out of breath and the area around them was nearly empty of passersby. Turning, she waited while Jareth walked on his knees up to her. He was sweating from the effort, the moisture making his blackened face more disreputable until he looked the villain she named him. Yet he was grinning.

"Clever girl. Here." He held out his top hat to her as he climbed gingerly to his feet. He could not quite hide the grimace at the pain the movement caused him. Glancing down, she saw blood soaking the edges of his torn trousers.

Guilt assailed her. "You're hurt."

He seemed to notice the wound for the first time and shrugged. "Nothing serious. And the price is small if it brings me closer to your forgiveness."

She swallowed and pushed his hat back at him.

He waved it away. "Keep it. You must know a good charity. Only tell me that I passed this test."

"You passed," she acknowledged as he tucked in his shirt. "Though I question who feels the more humbled at the moment."

His smile was wry. "I doubt you could surpass

me there. I will own that your test gave me more than a moment's pause."

"Yet you turned it into a game," she protested with reluctant admiration.

He spread his hands. "What would you have me do? Gnash my teeth and tear my clothes?"

She glanced pointedly at his bleeding knee. He chuckled. "Very well. You achieved a partial victory. Look on the bright side. You have two more opportunities to torment me. Now, if you don't mind, I prefer to return home and tend to my leg."

He bowed, then turned to go. Though he tried to hide it, she could see he was limping. Pride warred with guilt. She reached out a hand.

"Jareth, Mr. Darby, wait."

He looked at her askance.

"My carriage waits around the corner. Please let me see you home."

She thought he might refuse, but after a moment's hesitation, he nodded. She led the way.

Eight

Where does Lord Watkin find such unpleasant servants? Jareth wondered as he climbed stiffly into the lacquered Watkin carriage behind Eloise. The butler had been bad enough but the coachman was worse. He looked rail thin in the dark livery of the household, and his sharp blue eyes glared at Jareth as if the fellow suspected him of bloodying his knee just to wangle a ride.

The truth was that the blasted knee throbbed, and Jareth wasn't sure he could make it home on his own. As it was, he refused to let Eloise take him to his ugly little rooming house. He'd have her drop him at the Fenton, which wasn't too far. He only hoped he could hobble the rest of the way. He seated himself gingerly across from Eloise on the brown velvet upholstered bench and bit back a grunt of pain as the coach jolted forward.

She frowned, dark brows gathering. "Your knee appears to be swelling."

He leaned forward to check. The bleeding seemed to have stopped, but what he could see through the rent in his trousers was raw and puffy. He straightened and offered her an encouraging smile. "Ah well. You never said the tests would be easy."

Her exquisite eyes were clouded. "No, but I assure you, I did not intend to cripple you."

"Merely castrate me?"

He watched the color surge up her cheeks. "Surely any number of fathers and husbands have tried the same," she retorted, head high.

"No fathers," he replied, "and only one husband."

Her gaze focused on her gloved fingers as they worried the fabric of her soft navy gown. "Then the tale of your flight from London is true."

He leaned back, suddenly weary. "That depends. Which tale have you heard?"

She glanced up to meet his gaze head on. "I was told you tried to seduce Lady Hendricks and were driven off by her husband at gun point."

He could feel his face settling into forbidding lines. "That is a lie."

"Then what is the truth?"

The desire to tell her was strong, but he knew it would be a mistake. For one, he doubted she would see anything as the truth if it came from him. For another, he did not wish to start fresh gossip. "Did you meet Lord Hendricks before his happy demise?" he asked instead.

"I did not have the pleasure."

"It would not have been a pleasure, but that is not the point. Since you have not met any of the participants in that little drama except me, I suggest you talk with someone you trust who was about the *ton* at that time."

"Perhaps I shall," she replied. The touch of defiance in her tone told him he had been right about whom she would believe.

As she lapsed into silence, he found himself

watching her. That close, he could see feather-fine lines at the edges of her eyes and mouth. They made her look too serious for her age. Had he put them there? Or had something else troubled her since he'd known her? He had to keep his arm pressed against his side so as not to reach out and stroke away the worry. How sweet it would be to press his lips against her temple, to inhale the fragrance of her hair and feel it slide like satin through his fingers. But he was reformed and even if he weren't she would never forgive him if he trifled with her again.

But how tempting was that trifling. A poet had once claimed that a man never forgot his first love. Jareth was more willing to quote poets than agree with them, but he found this sentiment to be true. He remembered more about Eloise than any other woman he had dallied with: the first time they'd met, the first time he'd touched her hand, their first kiss, the look of sweet yearning in her eyes when they'd parted. He did not think it had been love that motivated him five years ago, but he would not be surprised had his feelings grown in that direction.

"You are staring at me," she said, shifting in her seat. "Am I so changed?"

"In some ways," he acknowledged. "In others, not at all. If I closed my eyes, we could easily be in Darby chapel again." She said nothing, but her reaction raised a chuckle from him. "Now you are staring."

She collected herself with obvious difficulty. "I am merely surprised that you remember."

"Of course I remember. Do you think me totally devoid of feeling?" When she did not answer, he shook his head. "I am not the monster you want to paint me, Eloise."

"Yes, you claim to have changed as well."

"In that, I have not changed. I'm no more a monster now than I was then."

She stiffened in her seat. "Then why did you leave me?" she blurted out.

"Madam," he replied, "I was driven off by a pitchfork."

"By someone else," she protested, leaning toward him as if intent on making her case. "Not by me. Were you so faint-hearted that you could not return to me later?"

The view down her bodice was enchanting, but he forced himself to sit back, cursing his role as gentleman. "May I remind you that I was wounded? It took some time and a great deal of fabrication to heal my posterior and my brother's suspicions." And even as he said it, he realized he had been only partially successful. If Adam hadn't suspected, Eloise's name would never have appeared among his effects.

Eloise was watching with equal suspicion. "Then your family knew about our assignations?"

"Not everything," he assured her. "The Darbys have ever kept their own council. Father insisted on it. He had high expectations of all of us. Adam was to be the mighty earl, Justinian the lofty scholar, and Alex the stalwart soldier."

"And what of you?" she asked softly.

He shrugged. "I'm the wastrel. Every family has to have one. Look in Debrett's."

She shook her head. "I sincerely doubt that the book of the English peerage covers that. But even if your family expected no better of you, how did you manage to explain your wound?"

He felt a grin forming. "I told them I fell from my horse and landed in a bramble patch. Adam was irritated that a Darby would be so ham-fisted, Helena was embarrassed to think of what the other titled families in the area might say if the matter became known, and Mother was sympathetic that her baby had been injured."

"Did no one question you?" she asked with a frown.

"Dr. Paxton pointed out how miraculous it was that none of my exposed skin had a scratch, but no one seemed to notice that discrepancy. I paid my valet to hide the fact that neither my trousers nor my small clothes had a mark on them."

Her frown deepened. "So you escaped censure, unscathed."

"Why does that disturb you? Neither of us would have wanted to be forced into marriage that young."

"No," she said, turning her gaze to the window. "Of course not."

He frowned. "Is that what this is all about? Did you expect me to offer?"

Her laugh was bitter. "Oh, indeed, no. Not Jareth Darby. Everyone knew you were only after fun. Why would I be so foolish as to believe you cared for me?"

Her censure stung. "I cared. I admired you greatly."

"Yet you simply left?"

He doubted she knew how young and vulnerable she sounded. In fact, her manner reminded him of the time they'd first met under the oak.

He softened his tone. "I never promised to stay. I thought I made that clear."

She sighed. "You may have said the words. I doubt that I listened. Your actions made me feel as if I were different from the others I knew you must have wooed. I thought I was special to you. I thought you loved me."

He could barely resist the urge to gather her in his arms. Speeches he had used to advantage in the past tumbled through his mind, but he rejected them all. She deserved better. She deserved the truth.

"I'm sorry, Eloise," he said. "It was never my intent to hurt you."

The carriage slowed then, and she seemed glad for the excuse to break his gaze and peer out. "We are nearing the Fenton Hotel," she murmured, her voice husky with emotion. "You are not staying with your brother?"

"My usual rooms are being remodeled," he lied. "Besides, I shall be returning to Somerset shortly, when my business in London is accomplished."

She made a noncommittal noise as the coachman climbed down to open the door and lower the step.

"When may I expect the second test?" he asked as he stiffly rose.

"Soon," she said, still avoiding his gaze. "I need time to think."

He hid a smile. It appeared his cooperation had been more effective than he had hoped. Perhaps gaining her forgiveness would not be so difficult after all. "Of course. I am at your disposal, Miss Watkin."

He clambered down, leg protesting, then turned to bid her farewell. "Perhaps we will see each other about town."

"Perhaps," she allowed, once more distant.

"I hope we can be civil?" he tried.

She nodded, but her look was far away. "Yes, civil. I think I can manage civil, Mr. Darby."

He bowed and the coachman set about his duties of raising the step and closing the door. Jareth raised a hand in salute as they drove off. Then he limped around the hotel to the seamier part of London.

His knee, he found once he reached the dark little room, was merely raw. A good cleansing and a compress made from one of his monogrammed handkerchiefs dressed it nicely. His trousers, however, were ruined. A shame, as that meant he had only three left—the dove gray, the blue velvet, and his chamois pair. He could only hope he could get the dirt out of his coat. It was one of four left to him.

He congratulated himself on being once more immaculate as he made his way back to Mayfair. He was pleased to find his brother at Darby House and enjoying a late luncheon.

"Ah, Jareth," Justinian greeted. "Have Baines fill you a plate. I can wait."

The footman hurried forward to comply. He piled up the bone china plate with shaved beef, lamb brisket, and poached salmon, and passed the board with sundry breads and cheeses. The fellow had evidently noticed how Jareth had been eating, for the platter groaned under the weight. Did he truly appear so starved? The grim reminder of his circumstances nearly turned his stomach, but he allowed the footman to place the food before him, spreading his damask napkin with every intention of doing the repast justice.

"What have you been up to all morning?" his brother asked.

"Entertaining Miss Watkin," Jareth said, between mouthfuls. "And if you hear rumors to the contrary, please deny that I have typhus."

Justinian choked.

Hoping to forestall questions, Jareth went on to tell his brother of the morning's escapades. Justinian shook his head as he finished.

"It must have been quite amusing," his brother said. "But I fail to see how you convince the *ton* you are changed if you appear to be chasing after Miss Watkin."

"I needn't convince the *ton,*" Jareth replied. "I merely need to convince Miss Watkin. You wished me to gain her forgiveness, did you not? This was her price, at least in part."

"I shudder to think what else she would have you do."

"Only two more such tests, the content of which are a strictly guarded secret. I begin to believe not even Miss Watkin knows what they are yet."

Justinian frowned. "She seems intent on making you pay. I take it you have remembered when you wronged her. What exactly passed between the two of you?"

Jareth paused. "Do you know, Justinian, I ask myself the same thing?" He started to explain the situation to his brother, then remembered the footman standing silently at the sideboard. He doubted Justinian would hire jabbermouths, but

Eloise seemed so intent on keeping their liaison secret that he could not trust speaking of it before anyone. She would never forgive him if she thought he'd spread gossip.

"I thought I was the only one injured," he told his brother, purposely keeping the matter vague. "Yet she seems incensed by the memory."

Justinian obviously had no concerns about the silence of his staff on family matters. "Incensed? Why? I cannot imagine you would press a woman to accept your advances. God knows, you have precious little need with the numbers who throw themselves at you."

Jareth frowned. Had he pressed Eloise into their ill-timed passion in the hayloft? He could remember the scene all too easily. Their courage in meeting had been growing; she had managed to slip away during the day this time, but insisted that she could only stay a moment. As had been happening frequently of late, he had found his time with her maddeningly short and had followed her back to the stable.

"Are you mad?" she whispered when she'd seen him in the breezeway between the stalls. "Do you have any idea what will happen if we are caught?"

He hadn't cared. Coaxing and crooning, he'd lured her up into the loft. Sweet kisses melted in the fire of their embrace. Going beyond kissing had seemed natural, right, the culmination of his dreams.

When the deed was actually accomplished, however, the passion on her beautiful face had broken for a moment into fear. At the time he had put it down to a fear of getting caught and kissed the look away. But if in fact she had been too afraid of him to say no, it might explain the reactions she had to him now.

"Jareth?" his brother urged, setting down his nearly empty cup of tea. "Answer me. Do you have more to apologize to Miss Watkin for than you originally thought?"

He shook his head. "I am no longer certain."

"What does Miss Watkin say?"

"She makes veiled hints but says very little."

His brother looked thoughtful, reminding Jareth of the scholar Justinian had once been. "Perhaps you should attempt to speak with Lady Hastings. She knew Miss Watkin at school, did she not?"

Jareth nodded. But he made his brother no promises. The Marchioness of Hastings would have sooner spit in his eye as give him the time of day, and he knew it. It was a very good thing Justinian hadn't added her to the list, or he'd be sunk.

But the idea of understanding what drove Eloise was a good one. He wanted to know what she held against him, why their past seemed so painful to her. Surely that could help him persuade her to forgive him.

Yet something told him that, in wanting to learn more about Eloise, he had another motive entirely.

Nine

Eloise also considered her motivations. Teaching Jareth a lesson was harder than she had thought. He reacted unexpectedly. He had experienced the humiliation and turned it into a merry prank. He had discussed their past as if it meant as much to him as it did to her, only to turn around and deny the very things she'd thought they'd shared. How could she possibly understand such a man?

She was more concerned, however, that what she did not understand she found strangely appealing. He was witty as always; she found it difficult to frown at his jests. There was no denying his sense of the ridiculous, and she envied him his ability to laugh at difficult circumstances.

She also could not deny his attractiveness. Even dirtied and bloodied, he'd been adorable. Sitting in the coach, it had been all she could do not to reach across and smooth down his pale hair. She had always thought a man's hair would be somehow rougher than a woman's, but Jareth's had always felt like satin. Would it still feel so good?

She shook herself. She could not be so foolish as to fall under his spell again! She must remember why she had set herself on this path of righteousness. His betrayal was a fact. His dalliance with other women was legendary. Even if his reformation was true, he had a great deal for which to atone.

"One part of our conversation truly puzzles me," she confided in Cleo the next afternoon as she visited her friend in the sunny sitting room of the Hastings's townhouse. "He suggested that I ask someone else about his affair with Lady Hendricks. How could that help him?"

"I cannot see that it would," Cleo replied, spreading her spring green gown to settle herself more comfortably on the rosewood settee. "Besides, you hardly have to ferret out the information. The gossip is so rampant now that he has returned that anyone could tell you the tale."

"Too many would be happy to tell me," Eloise confirmed. "How could I be certain what they say is the truth?"

Cleo nodded. "I have heard six versions of the story already. Lord Nathaniel told me one just before you called."

Eloise paused in the act of straightening the lace collar of her lilac cotton gown to smile. "Lord Nathaniel was here?"

"Indeed. I take it you had not seen him recently?"

"Yesterday, after I gave Mr. Darby his test."

Cleo frowned. "Had he heard about your escapades?"

"He did not mention it, and I think it likely he would have done so if he had heard. I suppose, however, it is only a matter of time before the *ton* begins to talk of it. We were rather conspicuous."

"Lord Nathaniel will not mind," Cleo predicted. "He is utterly devoted to you."

Eloise made a face. "So devoted that he has yet to propose! I tell you, Cleo, the man is impossible to pin down. He alludes to his feelings for me constantly, yet when I press him even the least bit, he backs away like a hound from a snarling cat."

"He could speak of little else but your qualities while he was here," Cleo insisted. "Surely if you are intent on having him, you have only to exert yourself."

Eloise sighed. "I have exerted myself as much as I am willing to, I assure you. Perhaps I am not as intent as I thought."

"Why?" Cleo demanded. "Eloise, I thought you had forsaken the game of leading gentlemen on."

"I have!" Eloise protested. "I did not toy with Lord Nathaniel's emotions. I wished his suit. He is handsome enough in his own way, congenial, good-hearted. Yet I cannot help but feel that something is missing in our times together."

"Such as?" Cleo prompted with a frown.

Eloise licked her lips, almost afraid to say the words aloud. "Such as love." When Cleo regarded her, head cocked so that her cinnamon hair fell over one ear, she hurried on. "Do I not deserve love, Cleo? Would you have me settle for less?"

"Never," Cleo swore, reaching out to touch Eloise's arm. "Of course you deserve love. But I fear for you, Eloise. I thought you cared for Lord Nathaniel, and now it seems your feelings have cooled. He has not changed. What has changed is the fact that Jareth Darby has returned."

"That is quite enough," Eloise informed her, feeling a sudden chill. She pulled her cashmere shawl more firmly about her shoulders. "I do not allow Jareth Darby to dictate my life or my relations with other gentlemen."

"I certainly hope not. By the by, Lord Nathaniel thinks Mr. Darby every bit the villain we do. He said as much when he told me the story about Lady Hendricks."

"What exactly had he heard?"

"The usual—that Lord Hendricks caught Mr. Darby seducing Lady Hendricks and drove him off at gunpoint. Only in his story, Mr. Darby struck Lord Hendricks from behind to make his escape."

"Poppycock," Eloise pronounced. "Jareth may be a rake, but he's no coward."

"He ran away from a child with a pitchfork," Cleo reminded her.

Eloise wrinkled her nose. "That wasn't cowardice. That was common sense."

Cleo raised a ginger brow. "You are defending him."

Eloise felt herself color. "I am merely seeking the truth, and I do not believe that story of striking Lord Hendricks is true. That is not the same as believing Mr. Darby innocent."

"Perhaps not," Cleo allowed, but the look in her dark eyes told Eloise she was not convinced. "And perhaps I have the answer to your question as to who could tell you the truth of the matter. Margaret, Lady DeGuis, should have been on the *ton* the year he was disgraced. We could ask her."

Eloise smiled. "Lady DeGuis is not known for her tact."

"No, but she is known for telling the truth," Cleo replied with a twinkle in her eye. "She is coming to visit this afternoon. If you wait, you may have your answer."

Eloise waited, but the answer was not what she expected. Then, of course, things were often not as one expected when one conversed with Lady DeGuis.

Margaret had inspired the *ton* as a true Original for many years. She was honest, even when it was not circumspect to be so. She lived by her convictions, no matter the cost. Tall and solidly built, she had thick, coarse hair with more silver than black even though she was less than ten years Eloise's senior. By far her most notable feature, however, was her loud, joyful laugh, which was the first thing Eloise heard when she posed her question about Jareth and Lady Hendricks.

Cleo exchanged surprised glances with Eloise. "You find the situation humorous, Lady DeGuis?"

Margaret chuckled. "And you do not, Lady Hastings? A renowned rake riding to the rescue? Surely you can appreciate the irony."

Cleo frowned while Eloise interjected, "Riding to the rescue? I fail to see how adultery qualifies him for sainthood."

Margaret raised a feathery silver-black brow. "Who said adultery was involved?"

"Oh, everyone," Cleo put in as Eloise frowned in confusion.

"Then everyone is wrong," Margaret proclaimed. "Which does not surprise me. The *ton* at times has no more sense than a flock of turkeys."

"If Jareth Darby wasn't having an affair with Lady Hendricks," Eloise said, "why was he forced to flee London?"

"No doubt because Lord Hendricks was out for blood." Margaret shook her head. "Perhaps I should start from the beginning. Cecilia, Lady Hendricks, attended school with me. We were fairly close and kept in touch during our debuts. She was sweet natured and blessed with a lovely head of golden curls. Her besetting sin was her need for notoriety. I warned her not to marry Lord Hendricks but his title and fortune blinded her to his faults."

"What do you mean?" Eloise probed.

"He beat her whenever he drank, and he drank to excess."

Eloise cringed, and Margaret gave a tight-lipped smile. "You know I cannot abide wrapping the dark in clean linen, Miss Watkin. The story of Cecilia Hendricks isn't a pretty one. She was trapped in a marriage that I am convinced would have been the death of her, if it hadn't been for the championing of Jareth Darby."

"Unlikely hero," Cleo muttered.

"I cannot agree," Margaret said. "Darby has ever been kind to the ladies, the lovely and those less favored. But by far the best thing he ever did was take up with Lady Hendricks. He had flirted with her before her marriage, of course. It should not be surprising that he came to her rescue that particular night."

"Why exactly did she need rescuing?" Cleo asked suspiciously.

"Her husband had at last shown his true colors. He got drunk at the Duchess of Richland's ball and shoved his wife down a flight of stairs."

Eloise gasped and heard Cleo do likewise.

Margaret nodded. "You may well look shocked.

It was horrible. Unfortunately for Cecilia, there were few nearby at the time to see her. Darby was one. He insisted on taking her home alone. Only he did not take her home right away."

Eloise knew she must have turned white. "He took advantage of her in that state?"

"Do not believe it for a minute," Margaret insisted. "No woman would be in the mood for romance after being bruised and banged about. Cecilia wrote me afterward. She went with him to the Fenton, where he was staying. He apparently hoped to keep her safe from her husband and urged her to leave the fellow altogether. Cecilia still thought she might make amends, as if she had done anything wrong. She insisted on returning home, then thanked Mr. Darby with a hug. Lord Hendricks found them together in her dressing room, locked in that embrace."

"And Jareth Darby left her to face the monster alone," Eloise murmured, seeing all too easily a mirror to her own life.

Margaret chuckled. "Actually, he planted the miscreant a facer. Cecilia insisted that he flee. She took the first ship for Canada. She writes me regularly. She is a painter now and quite happy about it."

"Then Mr. Darby is the hero after all?" Cleo said incredulously.

"In Cecilia Hendricks's eyes he is."

"That does not exonerate his other dalliances," Cleo insisted. "I still say he is a rake and a scoundrel."

"A rake, perhaps, but not a scoundrel," Margaret maintained. "I rather like his dash. Pity he's infected with the Darby pride."

Eloise wasn't sure that pride was his motivation. But then, she couldn't say what was. She left Cleo's with too much on her mind.

She and Cleo had vouchers for Almack's that night. Struggling as she was to see Jareth in the new light Lady DeGuis had offered, she considered staying home. Unfortunately, she was afraid to think how the patronesses might respond if she did not appear. Her reputation was much improved from last Season, it was true. But if her stunt on St. James had become known as she suspected, she would be better to go brave it out, behave like a lady, and put the rumors to rest.

Unfortunately when she arrived at Almack's beside Cleo and Leslie, she found it difficult to behave.

For one thing, Lord Nathaniel followed her about like a child's wooden pull toy. As she had begun to realize that what they felt for each other was not the kind of love upon which one built a marriage, she was no longer certain how to respond to his attentions. She thought she should give him the opportunity to declare his feelings, in case they were stronger than she suspected. Yet when she attempted to encourage him, he immediately paled, stammered, and offered to dash off for refreshments, her shawl, or one of her friends.

She would have liked nothing better than to sit him down and demand to know his intentions toward her. Unfortunately, she could hardly do so in so public a place as Almack's and she wasn't sure he wouldn't faint if she attempted the discussion in private. Her frustration was harder and harder to hide, and she was certain it showed in her face and conversation.

She also found it difficult to behave as some might have expected on the dance floor. Lady Jersey had insisted on a number of quadrilles, and Eloise loved dancing to the fast-paced music. While other ladies complained of the exertions, she delighted in the freedom. Lord Nathaniel seemed mildly concerned with her dancing and when he did not offer a second set, she promptly requested Lord Hastings to lead her out.

She had found partners for three quadrilles and a country dance when she spotted Jareth. Then it was even harder to behave. How could she act civilly toward him when he persisted in flaunting his dalliances? His partner was Portia Sinclair, and it was easy to imagine that he was bent on seduction. Why else would he smile in so charming a manner that the light shone from his blue eyes? Why would he allow his hand to brush her gloved arm? Why would he bend near as if to whisper into her tiny ear?

And Portia seemed just as bent on attracting attention. Miss Sinclair had outdone herself. Her apricot-colored gown was so sheer as to be nearly transparent, her lashes obviously blackened, and her lips rouged. She looked ripe for the plucking, and Jareth looked all too eager to sample the fruit.

He was wearing the blue velvet coat and trousers again and the richness of the color only made him look more opulent. Portia was obviously captivated. Why could the girl let herself gaze at Jareth so heatedly? Could she not tell that her skirts kept brushing his stockinged calves? Did she not see the fans plying as they passed, hear the gossip, smell the whiff of censure? The girl was out to ruin herself and Jareth in the process.

Eloise started. Was she actually concerned about how Portia's attentions could affect Jareth's reputation? Surely there was no need. His reputation for seduction needed no embellishment. And if he had truly reformed, wouldn't he stay away from the ladies' lures? And why should she care either way?

Unfortunately, she found that she cared all too much.

Ten

Jareth had to remind himself that he was reformed every time Portia Sinclair brushed her lithe body against his. Surely this was some sort of test. He'd only recently become reacquainted with the Bible, as Eleanor had taken to reading passages aloud on the evenings they did not go out. However, he was certain the story of the prodigal son did not end in forty days of temptation in the desert.

Yet Portia Sinclair seemed determined to test him. She was lovely, she was intelligent, she was vivacious, and most of all she seemed to have lost all interest in the major and was directing her youthful energies toward capturing him instead.

Take now, for instance. They had just finished a staid country dance that should never have winded a young lady like Portia, yet she used fatigue as an excuse to lean against him as he led her to an innocuous sofa to rest. Her gloved hand lingered in a caress on his arm as he straightened. Her smile seemed to promise more. Part of him was only too happy to oblige.

Yet he could not shake the feeling that something was wrong with the delightful Miss Sinclair. At times her attentions seemed almost desperate, as if much more were at stake than a mere flirtation. Her soft gray eyes held a longing that did not seem to have anything to do with her attraction to him.

He also could not understand why her stepmother, who chaperoned her tonight and kept casting them glances from across the room, allowed her to behave with such familiarity. Portia was hardly subtle. Already brows were being raised. Other mothers kept their daughters safely at their sides as he passed. Why hadn't her stepmother noticed Portia's fascination with him and come to drag her away?

Of course, someone else had noticed and he had to admit that the fact was unaccountably pleasing. Several times his gaze had been drawn to Eloise. Each time she had looked away with a blush, but not before he'd seen the speculation in her green eyes. She thought him enamored of Portia. A shame Eloise would not believe him if he told her that he found himself far more enamored of her.

He had spent the better part of the last two days trying to understand why Eloise was so chary of their past. Against his instincts, he'd called on Lady Hastings, but she had refused to see him. He had found several of Eloise's classmates, using various pretexts to call on them, but none seemed willing to volunteer information. He could tell they admired her; indeed, some seemed to envy her beauty, fortune, and wit.

If tonight were any indication, her popularity had only increased since their walk down St. James the day before. Lord Nathaniel was in evidence, fawning over her hand far more often than

Jareth thought necessary. He also spotted several other gentlemen showing interest.

They brought her refreshments. One hurried to fetch her paisley shawl from the cloak room, as if she needed anything to cover the fetching saffron confection she wore. Another insisted upon procuring a fan and fluttering it before her to cool her from the dance. Jareth would have far preferred to watch the heated blush rise up her well-molded bosom to her neck and cheeks.

He had to be content to watch her moving instead. Her hand was constantly in demand. Yet through all the adulation, she smiled graciously and danced gracefully. She did not seem to play favorites—bestowing as welcoming a smile on her first partner as the ones that followed. As far as he could see, no woman in the room could match her for beauty and poise and he knew few could match her in intelligence and breeding.

So, if she were this popular and worthy, why hadn't some fellow snatched her up in marriage?

"Mr. Darby, you are not attending."

He blinked and focused on Portia below him on the sofa. Her hand rested on the empty spot beside her as if she invited him to join her. He remained standing.

"Forgive me, Miss Sinclair," he said, inclining his head. "Your celebrated beauty made all else pale in comparison."

"Fie," she declared, rapping him lightly on the arm with her lace fan. "You, sir, were not even looking at me."

He rattled off his usual excuse for looking elsewhere. "Only because I carry your image in my heart. I see you in every marvel of nature, in every classical work of art." Even as he spoke, his gaze was drawn back to where Eloise was dancing in another quadrille. While the other dancers looked breathless or jerked through the steps, she alone accomplished the quick movements with the beauty and energy the dance required. His mouth curved in a smile of appreciation.

"Perhaps you should simply seduce *her.*"

Jareth's smile froze in place. "I beg your pardon?"

Portia trilled a laugh. "I wish I had a mirror that I might show you your face, Mr. Darby. I vow I have shocked you."

"And I vow that was your intent," Jareth replied with a rueful shake of his head. "You are a shameless baggage, Miss Sinclair."

"And you delight in it, Mr. Darby. Come, you know you do."

She was purposely baiting him. Once he would have been only too happy to take her up on the challenge shining from those changeable eyes. Tonight, he found his interest waning. Best to make his excuses while he still could.

"I did once," he agreed. "And I would be a hypocrite if I now maligned you. However, with the idea that I have been too obvious in my admiration, I shall withdraw."

She was instantly piqued, mouth turning down in a pout, and rapped him far less lightly to show her displeasure. "Nonsense, sir. Would you leave me alone in my weakness?"

He wanted to do just that but her statement arrested him. The words were hauntingly familiar. He had a sudden image of another face, battered and bruised, soulful gray eyes gazing up into his as he escorted her from the Richland townhouse.

"You would not leave me alone, Darby? Not until I can steel myself to face him again?"

He shook himself. This was hardly the same situation. Portia Sinclair did not need his help as Lady Hendricks had done. The girl was merely trying to be coy. Very likely it was his imagination that saw despair in her actions. Yet even as he tried to convince himself, he felt his smile strain.

He bowed. "You underestimate your own strength, my dear," he told her. But as he straightened to leave her, she reached out a hand to stop him. Her eyes were troubled, her golden brows drawn tight over her pert nose.

"You *are* after Eloise Watkin, aren't you?"

He drew himself up straighter, but she clung to him. His pointed look to where her fingers gripped his wrist forced her to release him. "May I point out, Miss Sinclair," he said stiffly, "that my intentions are none of your affair?"

"I am merely concerned for you," she protested, returning to her pretty pout, but this time with obvious difficulty. "She has encouraged several gentlemen, only to reject them when they proposed. I should not like to see you served likewise."

Was this the reason Eloise had yet to wed? Were her standards too high? She'd had the best in him, and the rest were not up to scratch. He smiled inwardly. Even he could not believe that. Certainly any number of gentlemen possessed greater fortunes, families, or figures than he did. With her assets, she could have had her pick. "I cannot see Miss Watkin as a jilt," he informed Portia. "Very likely the other gentlemen were found lacking."

"And you think you would not suffer that fate?" She shook her head at such arrogance. "Do not let the challenge blind you to her faults."

"Your concern for me is touching, but I assure you I have overcome any blindness I might have had when it comes to women."

She paled, and he suspected it was because he had implied he could see through her ruses as well. He did not give her time to protest further but turned his back and strode away.

He did not attempt to refresh himself with Almack's infamous weak lemonade, although he did sniff the punch available that night in case some industrious soul had kindly spiked it with more palatable ingredients. Unfortunately, he could detect only the strong odor of rose water. Of course, it could have come from the lady who leaned provocatively past him as he stood beside the refreshments. He purposefully moved on.

As he did so, he considered Portia's words again. She obviously thought to warn him away from Eloise. He had no intention of giving up his pursuit until he had won Eloise's forgiveness, but Portia had no way of knowing that. Yet even if Eloise had forgiven him that night and freed him to pursue other women, he wondered whether he'd have the interest. He'd already decided she was the most interesting and worthy woman about the *ton* that Season. Why should he settle for anything less?

Curious about his own reactions, he tried dancing with several of the other ladies present. The first was so nervous that she tripped over her own feet and fell neatly into his arms on the dance floor. She fled in mid-set, upsetting the pattern of the dance and forcing him to quit the floor. The second refused him with a sniff of her aristocratic nose. He spotted Lady Hastings nearby, smiling with obvious satisfaction, and wondered whether she'd had anything to do with the refusal. The third accepted his offer and acquitted herself well, but he felt no more than a momentary spark of interest. So much for his pursuits.

He decided he had better be sociable and did his duty by dancing with ladies who did not have partners. Their mothers or chaperones quickly claimed them afterward, as if he would ravish them in the middle of Almack's crowded dance floor. He wanted to laugh. Only one woman in the hall held his interest and she wanted nothing to do with him.

But as the musicians tuned up for the next set, he found himself drawn to her side.

"May I have this dance, Miss Watkin?"

She stiffened as she turned to acknowledge him. "Mr. Darby. I thought you were otherwise engaged."

He followed her gaze to where Portia stood beside her stepmother. Both stared at him. Even from here, he could see that Portia bit her lower lip. It looked as if the girl was forming an attachment to him. He'd have to disabuse her of that notion. He started by ignoring her.

"If you were watching me," he told Eloise, "you will note that I danced with other ladies before and after I danced with Miss Sinclair. In fact, I can safely say I have been the perfect bachelor this evening. Now I would like my reward."

She raised a brow. "You behave as you should, and you expect a reward?"

He was beginning to feel exactly that. "I behaved as Society dictates, ignoring my own desires. I think that should be rewarded."

She looked at him suspiciously from the corner of her green eyes. "And just what desires did you ignore that I should find you so praiseworthy?"

She most likely expected him to speak of his utter devotion to Portia. He bent his head closer to hers and drew her gaze to his own. "I wanted nothing so much as to cover your willing lips with kisses."

She swallowed, lashes fluttering lower. He could feel her breath come out in a soft gasp.

"However," he added, mindful of their audience, "I would settle for the next dance."

He wasn't sure how she might react. It wouldn't have surprised him had she bolted from the room. Instead, she raised her head to meet his gaze with defiance. "You are entirely too bold, Mr. Darby. I see no reason to encourage you."

"I have the best of reasons," he assured her. "If you refuse to dance with me, you shall have to sit out for the first time tonight."

Around them, couples lined up for another quadrille. He could see the debate going on in her mind. She obviously loved to dance, yet if she declined his offer, she would be forced by Society's rules to sit out this set. He nearly smiled as he found himself thankful for the rules for once. Yet, considering how she would react if she knew he thought he had the upper hand, he kept his face neutral.

She shook her head suddenly, as if disliking her own decision. "A devil's bargain, Mr. Darby, but I should have expected as much from you."

She glanced up at him, and he thought for a moment she would refuse after all. But she put her hand on his offered arm and he led her onto the floor to join the other couples.

He had hoped the dance might ease her tensions. However, she reverted to the regal air he had noticed their first night at the oak. She kept her head high as they passed, her gaze imperious when they took hands. Her movements were courtly, as if she knew she were on display and wanted to give no one any reason to find fault.

Given what little he understood of her feelings for him, such an attitude was obviously meant to put him in his place. The regal air was understandable at first, but as the dance progressed, he found himself more and more put out by it. Why couldn't he seem to charm her as he once had? Why didn't she respond to him as she used to? Had he lost his way with women that those he didn't want sought him out and those he wanted refused him? If that was reformation, he was ready to return to the streets.

Well, perhaps not that. However much she moved him, however little he moved her, he still had to earn her forgiveness. Surely he could only do so if she became more comfortable with him. Determined, he increased his charm.

He looked desolate when another fellow took her hand and brightened when she was returned to him. Whenever they were close enough, he murmured praises to her beauty, her poise, her grace. As they passed, his gaze sought hers until she was forced to acknowledge him with a movement of vivid green. He ran his finger along the back of her hand in a caress when they touched. He brushed her shoulder with his as they crossed.

His intent had been to make her more aware of him, but he found the tactic a double-edged sword. The more he brought her close, the more aware of her he became. When he passed her, he caught the scent of lilacs in her hair. When his fingers grazed hers he could imagine the silkiness of her skin and think of a dozen other places his fingers might play.

He must have had some effect on her because by the time the dance was over, they were both breathless. He wanted to talk to her then and there, but she seemed to sense it. Raising her head once again, she began to back away from him. He held onto her hand. Her gaze was determined, but he could imagine his own was just as implacable.

"Eloise," he started.

In the alcove above the door to the refreshment room, the musicians began the strains of a waltz. He could think of nothing finer than to have an excuse to hold her in his arms. He did not finish what he wanted to say. He didn't want to give her the opportunity to decline. He swept her into his arms and out across the floor.

Eleven

Eloise stared at him. What did he mean to hold her so closely in the middle of Almack's? He hadn't even asked her permission. Moreover, people were staring. She could see Cleo dancing nearby, face red in her fury at Jareth's actions. She should cry out, push away from him, force him to release her. Yet she could not seem to muster the desire.

Being in his arms again felt simply wonderful.

She marveled at it. How on earth could she feel so contented, dancing with one of the most renowned rakes in England? Yet she felt contented, and more. His hand on her waist was firm and warm. It moved in a slow caress of her back, raising a heat from deep inside her. His other hand held hers gently, cradled among his fingers, as if he cherished the touch as much as she did.

And his face. Here was something akin to the worshipful gaze she remembered. Only this time, it wasn't a youth who held her with his eyes, but a man. A man used to leading his life as he pleased. A man who had more than once damned the consequences to live on his own terms. A man who could have chosen any woman in the room, any woman in the world, and he had chosen her.

A man she would not be able to deny.

The thought shook her, and she stumbled. Jareth caught her smoothly.

"Easy now," he murmured. "You have no need to escape, Eloise. Nothing bad can happen in the middle of Almack's. Even *I* am not that wicked."

She nodded, not sure she believed him about his wickedness but perfectly willing to believe that none of the patronesses would allow him to sweep her away. Besides, somewhere on the dance floor were Cleo and Leslie, and surely she could count on them to assist her should he be so foolish as to break with propriety. Waltzing with him was perfectly safe. She forced herself to relax.

"Much better," he murmured as if to encourage her. "You are by far the best dancer here, you know. It is my pleasure to be your partner."

She did not want his praise to please her, coming as it most likely did with a price, but it pleased her nonetheless. She was sure she should deny it.

"Nonsense," she said. "Any number of young ladies dance better than I do. You should not offer me Spanish coin."

His eyes were warm. "Why would I falsely praise you?"

Why indeed? She shuddered to think of it. "You want my forgiveness. I have no doubt this is all part of your plan to weasel it out of me."

He raised a pale gold brow. "My plan? I thought I was the victim of your plan."

She snorted. "You have never been anyone's victim. You, sir, are the predator."

"And is it my fault there are so many delightful gazelle about? What is a proper lion to do?"

"You claim to have reformed."

"Ah, but I find that so very difficult when presented with such temptation." The teasing light faded from his eyes to be replaced by something else, something that warmed far more than her heart.

"You truly are beautiful, Eloise," he murmured.

She shook her head, trying in vain to clear the spell he was weaving around her. "And you are a flirt."

"Of course," he agreed readily. "I reformed from the sin of seduction. I never promised to give up the art of flirtation. Would you ask a master to stop painting?"

"No," she acknowledged. "And I will own that you are a master. But be warned, sir. I am on to your tricks."

"And I to your secret, madam."

She very nearly missed another step. "What are you talking about? Of course you know my secret. You *are* my secret. That is the entire reason you are forced to seek my forgiveness."

He smiled and shook his head. Then he drew her closer to whisper in her ear. "But you have another secret, my dear Eloise. I can feel it in the way you dance with me. I can see it in the way you look at me. At rare moments, I can even hear it in your voice. You don't hate me after all."

She wanted to deny it. She must deny it. She could not stand the gentle smile on his face as he pulled away to a discreet distance. Every time he was sweet, she felt the walls she had erected crumbling. She could not let him back into her heart. Her reputation would never survive a second betrayal. *She* would never survive such a betrayal.

Dancing in his arms was a mistake, she realized. Physical closeness had been her undoing once before. She had to get away from him and give herself sufficient distance to think clearly. As he turned them to the music, she brought her heel down hard on his toe.

Jareth grimaced, hopping back. His hand slipped from her back and she was able to pull her fingers from his grip, effectively stopping them in the center of the dance floor. She made her face the picture of dismay.

"Oh, Mr. Darby, I am so sorry. You should sit down."

"Another step like that one, madam," he gritted out, lowering his foot gingerly to the floor, "and I shall have to."

The music stopped then, but not before the other couples began casting them curious glances. Eloise smiled sweetly. "Would you like me to escort you to a chair?"

"That should not be necessary," Jareth replied. He nodded to a gentleman passing them, then attempted to take her elbow.

Eloise dodged neatly. "Then I shall leave you to find your next partner."

He reached for her again. She stepped away, but this time she was not so lucky. Jareth's hand caught her wrist and he pulled her closer to him, shaking his head as if in reluctant admiration. "I want no partner but you."

"But we have already had two dances, sir," she pointed out, prying away his fingers. "You must be fair to the other ladies, who no doubt cry for your company."

He rolled his eyes. "They will survive. I will not."

"You most certainly will," Eloise said with a sniff. "But if you are so eager for my company, be at my home at three in the afternoon, the day after tomorrow, for your second test."

He bowed, but she thought she saw the slightest hint of disappointment in those clear blue eyes. He had thought her so easily manipulated that she would relent. She would show him just how wrong he was.

She spent the better part of the next two days trying to determine exactly what the test should be. She wanted to put him in his place once and for all. Unfortunately, nothing she could contrive seemed sufficient.

As she sorted through one Machiavellian strategy after another, her social life came to a grinding halt. She only half-attended to the discussion of her literary group on the novel they were reading, she forgot a riding appointment with several of her former classmates from the Barnsley School, and she was careless in her devotions.

It was apparent that even her father noticed her preoccupation.

"Is there something on your mind, Eloise?" he asked over the second course of dinner one night.

She smiled politely at him down the long table to the far end where he sat. "Nothing of import, Father."

She thought he offered a smile in return, but at that distance, it was difficult to tell. Though he did not question her further, she could not help but feel she had given him a poor answer.

She was also poor company for her callers. She barely managed to entertain her share of beaus, among whom was the ever-hesitant Lord Nathaniel. He had gone so far as to fervently press her hand and tell her again how much he admired her. Unfortunately, before she could tell him that she would prefer to have proof of something beyond mere admiration, he'd become so misty eyed that he had been forced to excuse himself, still without so much as a suggestion that he might wish to speak to her father.

She was just as glad. She wouldn't have known what to tell him. She would have to come to terms with their feelings for each other, and soon, but not until she had accomplished Jareth's comeuppance. This second test must not fail. She refused to have him turn the tables on her again. What she needed was an environment supportive of her goals, not his. Unfortunately, she wasn't certain such a place existed.

Her ruminations were interrupted Thursday afternoon by an unexpected caller.

"A Mrs. Sinclair, by her card," Bryerton told her from the doorway to the forward salon where she had gone to think. "She and Miss Portia Sinclair are waiting in the entry."

Meaning that he had found them wanting, Eloise thought as she lifted her lilac lustring skirts to descend the stairs. One could always tell Bryerton's opinion of their guests. Worthy people were ushered into the garden withdrawing room immediately. Less impressive persons might be allowed on the main floor. Only the questionable

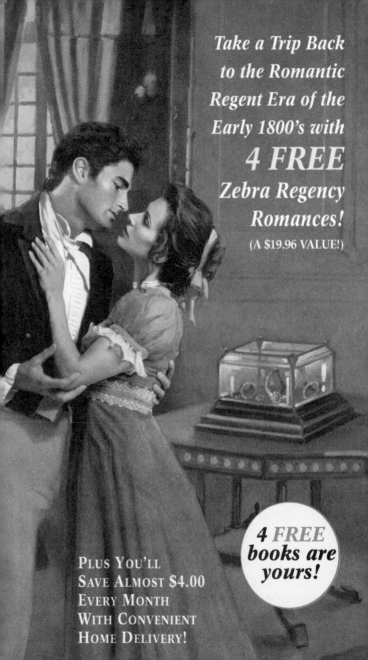

We'd Like to Invite You to Subscribe to Zebra's Regency Romance Book Club and Give You a Gift of 4 Free Books as Your Introduction! (Worth $19.96!)

If you're a Regency lover, imagine the joy of getting 4 FREE Zebra Regency Romances and then the chance to have these lovely stories delivered to your home each month at the lowest price available! Well, that's our offer to you and here how you benefit by becoming a Regency Romance subscriber:

* 4 FREE Introductory Regency Romances are delivered to your doorstep (you only pay for shipping and handling)

* 4 BRAND NEW Regencies are then delivered each month (usually before they're available in bookstores)

* Subscribers save almost $4.00 every month

* You also receive a FREE monthly newsletter, which features author profiles, discounts, subscriber benefits, book previews and more

* No risks or obligations...in other words, you can cancel whenever you wish with no questions asked

Join the thousands of readers who enjoy the savings and convenience offered to Regency Romance subscribers. After your initial introductory shipment, you receive 4 brand-new Zebra Regency Romances each month to examine for 10 days. Then, if you decide to keep the books, you'll pay the preferred subscriber's price, plus shipping and handling.

It's a no-lose proposition, so return the FREE BOOK CERTIFICATE today!

Say Yes to 4 Free Books!

Complete and return the order card to receive this $19.96 value, ABSOLUTELY FREE!

If the certificate is missing below, write to:
Regency Romance Book Club
P.O. Box 5214, Clifton, New Jersey 07015-5214
or call TOLL-FREE 1-800-770-1963

Visit our website at www.kensingtonbooks.com.

FREE BOOK CERTIFICATE

YES! Please rush me 4 Zebra Regency Romances (I only pay for shipping and handling). I understand that each month thereafter I will be able to preview 4 brand-new Regency Romances FREE for 10 days. Then, if I should decide to keep them, I will pay the money-saving preferred subscriber's price for all 4...that's a savings of 20% off the publisher's price. I may return any shipment within 10 days and owe nothing, and I may cancel this subscription at any time. My 4 FREE books will be mine to keep in any case.

Name _____

Address _____ Apt. _____

City _____ State _____ Zip _____

Telephone ( ) _____

Signature _____ RN082A
(If under 18, parent or guardian must sign.)

Terms and prices subject to change. Orders subject to acceptance by Regency Romance Book Club.
Offer valid in U.S. only.

lll..l..lll....lll.l.l.l.l.l..l.l.l.l.l.l..ll.l.lll..l

REGENCY ROMANCE BOOK CLUB
Zebra Home Subscription Service, Inc.
P.O. Box 5214
Clifton NJ 07015-5214

PLACE
STAMP
HERE

were left cooling their heels in the entry. She very nearly giggled remembering how long it had taken Jareth to make it past the front steps.

Portia and her stepmother were indeed standing in the entry. Portia was obviously uncomfortable. She kept shifting from foot to foot, the movements obvious in a green-sprigged muslin gown that barely reached her ankles. Her stepmother stood more calmly, stiff in a spruce gown with severe lines that still betrayed her bulk. Her dark gaze darted from portrait to footman to the door and back again in jerky movements as if she too were nervous.

"Mrs. Sinclair, Miss Sinclair," Eloise greeted them as she came down the stairs. "How nice of you to call. Will you join me in the sitting room?"

She led the way across the white-tiled entry to the opposite side where double oak doors opened onto a small receiving area. She perched on one of the hard-backed chairs and motioned Portia and her stepmother to chairs nearby. The girl sat on the edge of a chair and scooted it away from Eloise. It screeched as it crossed the edge of the Oriental carpet onto the hardwood floor. Eloise pretended not to notice, but Mrs. Sinclair grimaced and jerked her head as if to encourage Portia to begin.

Portia's smile was tight. "You must think me forward in coming to see you like this, Miss Watkin, particularly as we have barely been introduced. But after talking with my stepmother, I felt I must speak with you about a particular friend we have in common."

Eloise could not imagine who the girl could

mean. As far as she knew, they had no acquaintances in common. "Oh?" she prompted.

"Yes. Mr. Darby. Mr. Jareth Darby."

Eloise put on her most polite smile. "You have been misinformed, Miss Sinclair. Mr. Darby and I are not particular friends. We barely know each other." That was certainly true. She began to think she would never truly know him.

Portia blinked her soft gray eyes as if in confusion, exchanging glances with her stepmother.

"But he speaks so highly of you," Mrs. Sinclair put in firmly. "Naturally, we assumed . . ."

"Yes, well, now you know the truth," Eloise told her. "I daresay Mr. Darby has far more interest in Miss Sinclair than he has in me." She meant the sentiment to be encouraging but was surprised at how bitter it sounded. Portia apparently didn't find fault, however, for she blushed and lowered her gaze.

Mrs. Sinclair nodded. "I told her so."

Portia's blush deepened. "I should be quite flattered if that were true, Miss Watkin. I greatly admire Mr. Darby."

"He is a rare gentleman," Eloise allowed. "But I am afraid I can shed no more light on his interests. Was there anything else you wished to discuss with me?"

Portia toyed with the lace on her long, puffed sleeves while her stepmother leaned forward. "We also came to wish you happy," Mrs. Sinclair said, though the cheery words did not match the cool look in her gray eyes. "I believe I heard you are shortly to become Lady Nathaniel?"

Now *that* she must deny. All she needed was for the viscount to think she had set out to capture him. Admiration might be ladylike; outright entrapment certainly was not. Eloise shook her head. "I am certain no such announcement has been made."

Portia raised her head, gray eyes flashing. "Why the cad!" she cried. "I have witnessed Lord Nathaniel's devotion to you, Miss Watkin. He has never been so marked in his affections to another woman. If he should spurn you now, I would think him very callous indeed."

"He has not spurned me, I assure you," Eloise corrected her hurriedly. She began to think she would never make it through the conversation without starting or confirming gossip. "I consider him a very dear friend and would be delighted should he seek to further that friendship."

"Oh, how lovely," Portia replied happily.

"Yes, lovely," her stepmother purred. "Then, of course, you can have no interest in Mr. Darby." She smiled, but Eloise could not feel comforted. Mrs. Sinclair obviously considered herself subtle, yet in fact her aim was painfully clear. She wanted to make sure Eloise was happily occupied, leaving Portia an open path to Jareth. Eloise knew it was her duty to encourage the girl to look elsewhere.

"Yes, it is lovely," she agreed. "But I am certain one day I shall be wishing you happy, Miss Sinclair. You are having a marvelous Season. Any number of young men have shown interest, particularly that handsome Major Churchill."

Portia's hand froze on her sleeve.

Mrs. Sinclair's smile froze as well. "Major Churchill was recalled to the field."

The clock on the mantel chimed the half hour with a cheery note. Portia leapt to her feet. "Oh, look at the time! How remiss of us to keep you so late. We must be going."

Mrs. Sinclair rose more slowly. "Yes, we must. Good day, Miss Watkin. Give our regards to Mr. Darby, if you should see him."

She made it sound as if that were highly unlikely. Eloise did not argue the point, merely rising to see them out.

As she climbed the stairs again, she could only conclude that Jareth had made another conquest in Portia Sinclair. He even seemed to have won over the stepmother. Why did women persist in throwing themselves at him? Could no one else see him for what he was?

Perhaps she should turn it around. Could he not see the damage he did to the women with whom he dallied? If only she could show him without opening herself to the pain again. If only she could find another courageous woman who had been used and was willing to admit it.

Then she knew exactly what the second test should be. It would take some convincing to pull it off. But if she started now, she might be ready by tomorrow afternoon, Saturday at the latest.

Jareth Darby was about to be introduced to the evils of philandering by women who had experienced it first hand. She could hardly wait.

Twelve

Jareth presented himself at the Watkin townhouse exactly at three on Friday as requested. The two days had gone entirely too slowly for him. For one thing, he could not seem to forget how Eloise had felt in his arms as they danced. Indeed, the wondrous look on her face as he'd held her had raised in him such a fierce desire to protect her that he found it hard not to call on her sooner. Yet he sensed that if he called sooner, she would feel as if he were pursuing her, and he wasn't sure how she'd react to that pursuit.

Something was clearly troubling her. At first he had thought she feared that the *ton* might learn of their illicit affair. Then there was the issue of whether she actually feared him. Now he began to suspect that what she feared was forming a deeper attachment to him. Her heart had evidently been more involved in their earlier affair than he had thought, and she sought to protect herself from him this time.

None of his other ladies had ever pretended to love him. The idea that Eloise had loved him and might still be vulnerable to that emotion was surprisingly sweet. Yet he was not sure he was capable of yielding to the same emotion. He admired the

ladies with whom he dallied, cared about their
well being, but the soul-sharing love the poets
praised had never been his.

Yet he could not deny that what he felt for
Eloise was perilously close to that emotion. Certainly he could not escape her. Thoughts of Eloise
seemed to follow him by day and by night. He'd
smile at a pretty young miss only to notice that
her hair was not as lustrous as Eloise's. He'd engage a more seasoned lady in conversation and
find that her responses were not as witty as
Eloise's. He'd even gone so far as to visit one of
the more reputable gaming houses, where the
hostess had been willing to let him sample her
wares. To his surprise, he found himself uninter-
ested. Instead, he wondered how Eloise would feel
if she knew he was not as reformed as he claimed.

He couldn't even forget her through activities.
While he had learned the locations of some of
his old friends, he had not managed to call on
them. One was in Bethlehem mental hospital, another recuperating from a bout of gout, and the
rest happily married and raising children on various country estates. By the time the two days had
passed, he was more than ready for some excitement and could not imagine a better companion
in it than Eloise.

She looked ready for it. There was a decided
sparkle in those green eyes as the butler escorted
him into the pale room. She generally did not
dress with ostentation, but today her gown was a
simple calico frock with a practical green broad-
cloth spencer. The crisp lines of the gown, however, only served to call attention to her curves.

He bowed over her hand, allowing himself the

luxury of lingering over the salute. She did not pull away as quickly as she had recently. Surprised and pleased, he spread the tails of his navy coat and seated himself beside her on the sofa.

"And what delights have you planned for me today, madam?" he asked with a smile.

The sparkle grew more pronounced. "I am putting you to work, Mr. Darby, if you can find a suitable position."

He raised a brow. "What did you have in mind? Perhaps lady's maid?"

She shook her head. "Much too easy for you, I have no doubt. No, I wish you to assist me in doing charity work, at Comfort House."

"Comfort House?" He could not hide his grin. "It sounds as if I would fit in rather well."

She smiled. "I think you may indeed. Comfort House is a home for women who hope to leave a life of prostitution. Lady Thomas DeGuis and Mrs. Anne Turner arrange for the women to be taught skills to make an honest way in the world."

"I see," Jareth said, though in truth he did not. "And how might I assist?"

"That is what we must determine. I volunteer once or twice a week to teach the finer points of sewing. Do you have anything useful you could teach?"

He could see that she expected him to have no answer; those green eyes were far too wise. He licked his lips. "How to refuse a solicitation of sexual favors?"

That wiped the smile from her face. "Oh, really," she started. "I hardly think——." She stopped suddenly, cocking her head to regard him steadily. Black ringlets tumbled over her shoulders, making his fingers itch to stroke them. "Perhaps you could at that," she acknowledged. "I know Lady DeGuis laments the fact that the women of Comfort House are far too easy prey. Some men refuse to let them renounce their trade. And even when they find other employment, they are not treated fairly. Some employers even expect favors."

He had made the suggestion as a joke but if she approved of the idea, it might make this test all the easier to pass. "I would be delighted to teach your young doves how to make their way in the world without sullying their feathers."

She shook her head. "That is quite enough of your euphemisms. Lady DeGuis despises them. In fact, you had better behave yourself, Jareth. Lady DeGuis appears to admire you, but neither she nor Mrs. Turner will find your flirting the least bit amusing. And the women of Comfort House have had too much experience with men like you to appreciate the finer points of your address." She seemed to have convinced herself, for she straightened and smoothed down her calico skirts. "Yes, you will not find this test easy to pass."

"And what is the test, precisely?" he asked, leaning back to cross one booted leg over the other. "That I shall be able to resist the blandishments of the various tenants? I assure you, if you are there, I will have eyes for no one else."

"Nonsense. And I will be there. You may count on it."

"And the test?"

"Is of your kindness. Demonstrate to my satisfaction that you are able to treat these women with respect and compassion." She looked him in the eye, the green of her gaze gone suddenly flat with determination. "Notice the prefix on the word, if you will. Com-passion, sir, not passion."

"I shall be a plaster saint," he promised.

He found those words difficult to live by when he accompanied Eloise in her carriage to the house that afternoon. There were beautiful women everywhere. Cherub-faced girls peered at him from between the balusters on the stairs. Experienced courtesans strolled past in the uncarpeted corridor, their assets readily displayed, their interest in him obvious. While none stirred him to the depths that Eloise did, he would have to be the plaster saint he had promised to be not to look appreciative. How was he to prove himself kind and respectful when the very fruit of womanhood was laid out before him, like a buffet table groaning with delights?

Eloise was obviously expecting him to fail for he felt her gaze on him from the moment they were met at the front door by Mrs. Turner. Eloise had told him the woman was the house chaperone, but it was plain to him that she had once plied the same trade as her tenants. With soft brown hair piled high on her head and warm brown eyes, she had not lost the seductive, hip-swinging walk of a woman used to attracting attention for a living. The drab brown gown did nothing to hide her considerable curves. However, her gaze was even more assessing than Eloise's.

"I don't know what I was thinking of to agree

to this," she told them both. "Mr. Darby, you are simply too pretty to be of use to us."

Jareth raised a brow. "Do you judge a book by its cover, madam?"

"No, thanks to her ladyship teaching us to read."

"I believe Mr. Darby means," Eloise put in kindly, "that you should try his skills before determining his usefulness."

Mrs. Turner snorted. "He could be the best teacher since the good Lord himself and I couldn't use him. Just look at him, Miss Eloise. He'll have them stacked six deep begging for favors."

The picture was infinitely satisfying, but he quickly wiped away the smile it brought to his face. "Would you prefer I grew warts? Perhaps crossed my eyes?"

That wrung a chuckle from her, and Eloise turned away as if to hide a smile. "I doubt you could make yourself homely enough for my needs," the woman told him. "But perhaps you might work after all, if you keep your wits about you. Just remember our goal, Mr. Darby. We want these women to earn a place in good society, not a spot in your bed."

He bowed. "I will endeavor to say nothing suggestive, madam."

She shook her head. "You don't have to try to be suggestive; that smile is enough. But very well. You can teach. I'll bring them to the dining room for you. It's the one spot we have that will hold most of them. I think we have a dozen on their feet today. This way."

"On their feet?" Jareth murmured to Eloise as

they followed their hostess across the darkly papered corridor to what had once been a formal dining room. The wallpaper had been covered with a wash of pink paint, but the worn red carpet beneath the long walnut table made the room look heavy and not a little shabby.

"Some of the women arrive ill or injured," Eloise whispered back as they took their places at the head of the thick-legged table and waited as Mrs. Turner left. "They remain bedridden until they are well or . . . leave another way."

Now she was using a euphemism. It obviously distressed her that the women might die from their trade. He wasn't sure he much liked the idea either. He had never considered the long-term prospects of a prostitute. Though some were surely well compensated, it appeared the pay was not generally commensurate with the risks of losing a place in Society or living without the benefit of laws protecting wives. Yet surely none of the comely lasses he'd seen here need fear such an ugly end.

He was less optimistic when Mrs. Turner had gathered his students. The youngest was perhaps twelve, the oldest twice his age. Faces that should be dewy with youth or soft from a well-lived life were hard. Eyes that should sparkle with delight were wary, nearly feral. He was the center of attention and, from the knowing smiles, no little speculation. Beside him, even Eloise had crossed her arms over her chest as if waiting for him to step over the line Mrs. Turner had drawn.

The house chaperone called the meeting to attention. "Ladies, we have a special tutor today. This is Mr. . . ."

"Jareth Darby," an older woman halfway up the table finished. "I know him."

Eloise glared at him, and he tried to look innocent. In truth, he did not recognize the woman, though perhaps when he'd last seen her, her graying hair had been another color, her gaunt form more rounded.

"I know him too," piped up a young redhead he would have been delighted to know just as she was. "He closed down Madam Benecia's four years ago."

"Bought out the entire house for two days and had every meal catered by Gunter's," a plump brunette said with awe in her voice. "All those lovely sweets. Best time we had in years."

Now Mrs. Turner was glaring at him as well. Jareth rose from his seat and raised his hands to forestall any other revelations. "Ladies, you are too kind. I admit to being a bit wild in my youth. However, like you, I am in the process of reforming my life."

A collective sigh rippled down the table. "Rotten luck," someone muttered. He did not have to look at Eloise to know she must be flaming.

"I am here today," he continued doggedly, "because Miss Watkin believes I may have some wisdom to impart to you as you return to Society. I am here to teach you how to refuse a man's advances."

As one, they frowned at him.

"Why would we want to do that?" a blonde asked.

"What have I been teaching you?" Mrs. Turner demanded, scowling at them. "You'll be going out to work. Sooner or later, some fribble is bound to ask for favors."

A plump brunette shrugged, allowing the sleeve of her worn gown to slip off a comely shoulder. "Easiest thing is to give it to him and get it over with."

"It might be easy at the time," Eloise put in. "But unless you think before acting, you may live to regret it."

Jareth thought he knew where she'd learned that lesson.

"Someone should have explained that to Mr. Darby," the older woman said.

Jareth bowed as they all joined her in laughter. "Yes, madam," he said as he straightened. "They should have. I fully admit to acting without considering the consequences. Because of that trait, I spent three long years away from family and friends. Even now, there are those who refuse to acknowledge me, women who cross the street lest the hems of their skirts touch me."

He had their attention now, including Eloise. "I had to lose my oldest brother and his wife and come close to losing my own life before I realized that friends and family are far too important to jeopardize on a whim. If I can help you secure and maintain a place in Society, among friends, I would be honored."

"Well, I was willing to listen to you when I heard you fed Gunter's to Benecia's girls," someone called.

"Tell us what we need to know, Mr. Darby," the redhead urged.

They all nodded. He could feel Eloise watching him.

"With pleasure, madam," he said with another bow. "But I shall need a volunteer."

Cries of willingness rang out around the table, and several of the women jumped to their feet.

He turned purposely to Eloise. "Miss Watkin? If you would be so kind as to assist?"

Thirteen

Eloise wasn't entirely certain what had happened in the last few minutes. Jareth's past should have made him universally recognized as a villain, yet he appeared to be the hero instead. He had woven his spell over all of them. And now he wanted her help?

He held out his hand palm up, smile gentle. "Please, Miss Watkin? It would mean the world to me."

The yearning look on his face, the soft tone of his voice, and the congenial words combined to remind her of an earlier time, a time when she would have done anything for him. Even though he asked a small thing, she wasn't sure she should encourage him by stepping back into that role.

The ladies at the table obviously could not understand her hesitation. They called encouragement to her or begged him to consider them instead.

"For pity's sake, Miss Eloise," Mrs. Turner muttered, leaning toward her. "Give the man your help before we have a riot."

She nodded in understanding. Much as she would have liked to refuse him, she could not let her confused feelings for Jareth disrupt Mrs.

Turner's plans. She put on a smile and accepted the strength of his grip to rise. Her hand felt tiny in his.

"Certainly, I will assist you, Mr. Darby," she said, meeting his gaze with a look of determination. "Anything to help the ladies of Comfort House."

He squeezed her fingers as if he understood that she wasn't doing this for him. Yet something in his gaze made her catch her breath. It was as if he appreciated that she would make such a sacrifice for others. When he released her to return his attention to the ladies at the table, she felt as if she'd lost a necessary crutch.

"Now," he began, "young ladies of the *ton* are not so much taught what I am going to teach you, but learn by necessity and example. For instance, I would suspect the lovely Miss Watkin has learned any number of ways to depress a gentleman's notions."

Not the least of which was a well-placed pitchfork. "I believe Mr. Darby has experienced a rather pointed demonstration of that fact," she replied with an over-bright smile.

His smile widened. "Indeed, Miss Watkin. Quite pointed. However," he gazed back at their rapt audience, smile fading, "I would hazard a guess that you are likely to meet unsuitable advances in less congenial places than a dress ball or musicale."

Rather insightful of him, Eloise thought, though a part of her maintained that he had come by the knowledge first hand.

"That's God's truth," someone put in.

"So, let us say," Jareth continued, holding them with his sharp blue gaze, "that you have been engaged to work at a house and the master proves himself more interested in your assets than your ability to polish silver. What do you do?"

"Give him what he wants and ask for the silver," the blonde cried out. Eloise bit back a smile at the ingenious answer. Amidst the laughter around the table, Jareth shook his head.

"I assure you that if you do, the lady of the house will likely have Bow Street after you, claiming you stole the silver. No, you must find a way to show your master you are not interested but keep his dignity intact."

The fellow took liberties and they were supposed to pamper his puffed up consequence? Eloise didn't much like the sound of that. Neither did some of the ladies, it appeared, for they were frowning again.

The older woman snorted. "Might as well ask for the moon."

"Not at all," Jareth assured them. "Let me demonstrate. Miss Watkin, if you would play the master, I will attempt to demur."

Eloise blinked. "I am to be the man?" she asked, knowing she sounded as surprised as she felt.

He grinned as if he too appreciated the irony. "Indeed. And I shall be the maid. Come after me, if you will, with licentious intent."

She could not help herself and burst out laughing. But Jareth merely cocked his platinum head and looked at her from under his brows. She shook her head and swallowed the last giggle.

"Very well," she agreed. She thought for a moment, then straightened her shoulders and deepened her voice. "See here, Miss Darby, I desire you to serve my needs."

"Knew a bloke once what talked just like that too," the redhead whispered loudly to the woman next to her.

Jareth rolled his eyes. "No, no, Miss Watkin. I said come *after* me. Attempt to inflict yourself upon me."

She felt the color rushing to her face. "Mr. Darby," she began heatedly but Mrs. Turner interceded.

"Perhaps I might try this one, Mr. Darby," she said, rising to step in front of Eloise. Left with no other choice, Eloise returned to her seat. Part of her was relieved; another part was curious as to what the house chaperone meant to do. To her surprise, Mrs. Turner threw her arms around Jareth, pinning the sleeves of his navy jacket to his chest and nearly knocking him off his booted feet.

"I have you now, my pretty," she claimed in a throaty whisper as she pressed him backward. "Give us a kiss."

Eloise had to bite her lips together to keep from laughing at the startled look on Jareth's handsome face. But his surprise was short lived. Falling into character, he made his face the epitome of outraged femininity. His voice came out a high falsetto. "I am a proper lady, Mr. Hothands. Release me at once."

"Like that'd work," the brunette grumbled.

Eloise too had her doubts. Mrs. Turner stood her ground, brown eyes hard.

"I pay your wages," the chaperone-turned-libertine snarled. "You do as I say."

"Not in this, I don't." Jareth turned his head to look at his audience and dropped his voice to its normal pitch. "And then you scream, ladies, and if he still doesn't release you, you bring your knee up thus."

Mrs. Turner winced even though he did not connect with her. Eloise could imagine that if a lady did connect with a gentleman in that area of his anatomy with sufficient force, she might indeed cause him a great deal of harm. A shame she hadn't known the trick five years ago, but, of course, she doubted she'd have wanted to use it on Jareth then.

"That won't help his dignity," someone pointed out.

"Indeed, it will not," Jareth agreed, moving out of Mrs. Turner's grip and straightening his white cravat. "However, what you do next will help him maintain his consequence. If you would collapse, Mrs. Turner?"

She obligingly crumpled to the floor, dark skirts pooling about her body. She added a convincing writhe for good measure. Several of the ladies rose to get a better view of her.

"Help, help!" Jareth called out in his falsetto. "The master is ill!" He lowered the pitch. "Then, when the other staff come to investigate, explain that you found the poor fellow twitching and moaning. With any luck, they'll call a physician and have the creature bled."

"Now that's nasty," the older woman said in obvious admiration.

Eloise could not be satisfied. "A charming example, Mr. Darby, but your plan will only work if the gentleman does not decide to get vindictive after he has recovered. What if he paints you as the villain? What if he claims you attempted to seduce him?"

He regarded her so intently that she could feel herself blushing. "In general, Miss Watkin, I believe most gentlemen will back away rather than be wounded again."

Now it was her turn to stare. Back away? That was exactly what he had done. She had always wondered why he had refused to return for her. When Cleo had forced him off with the pitchfork, was it his pride that had kept him away? She had not thought him such a peacock as that.

The others were no less skeptical of his claims.

"I've met too many blokes what wanted more than they could have," the redhead maintained. "What you did might work with some, Mr. Darby, but I think Miss Eloise has the right of it. Some fellows can be right ugly when they don't get what they want."

"Those fellows," Jareth told her, "are not motivated by lust. If you are faced with such a vindictive master, I advise you to quit the position as quickly as possible, even if you have to forego references."

"What if you're cornered? What if he forces you?"

Eloise wasn't sure who had asked the question, but when she looked down the table she saw only faces gone white. Several avoided her gaze. The idea that any of the women she had come to care for would be violated in such a manner was too hideous to contemplate. Yet they had obviously considered the possibility. The answer gravely concerned them all, and she did not know what to tell them.

Jareth had no such trouble. "Send me word," he said quietly, "and I promise he'll never trouble you again."

One by one, they nodded, and the color returned to their faces. Eloise turned away. His words were heroic, but she could not believe him. Yet if she denounced him, she would only frighten them again. Behind her, she heard Mrs. Turner return to her feet.

"Easy to say, Mr. Darby," the house chaperone cautioned, "but I wager you won't remember half these women when you leave here."

"You may be right," Jareth replied. "They may also forget all about my offer. So, let us discuss what else we can do to stop that problem before it starts. As I said, a gentleman who forces a lady generally isn't after her because of her beauty or seductiveness, he's trying to prove to himself that he's truly a man. Bullying is one way of proving that you are superior when you suspect you are quite inferior indeed."

Eloise knew she was staring at him again. She had not thought him capable of thinking through such sentiments. *Of course,* she reflected, *he could be referring to Lord Hendricks.*

"What you must do," he continued, "is make sure you do not allow yourself to fall into the clutches of such a bully. Generally, his actions will prove his motivation. However, you can take certain steps to ensure you do not give any gentleman the opportunity to gain the upper hand. Miss Watkin, what would you do if I asked you out walking one night?"

Eloise smiled sweetly. "I would tell you to go to blazes, Mr. Darby."

As several of the women chuckled, he grinned at her. "Precisely!" He turned to the ladies again. "That is the first rule to prevent dire occurrences. Go nowhere after dark with a man you do not trust."

"Or into an enclosed space like a hayloft?" Eloise suggested with false innocence.

His grin turned wry. "Right again. Furthermore, do not offer a kiss if you suspect more is wanted."

That hit closer to home than she liked. Had he laughed at her when she had given in so easily? Perhaps she should show him what she had learned from his earlier teaching.

"Do not believe pretty words until you have seen them put into practice," she countered.

"Can't we do nothing fun?" the brunette complained.

"Certainly," Jareth advised. "But I quite agree with Miss Watkin. Find a gentleman who proves himself trustworthy by his actions. Then believe it is your God-given right to be treated with respect." He gazed at Eloise, and she felt herself coloring again at the warmth she saw in the blue expanse of his eyes. "With respect and with tenderness. Accept nothing less, ladies, and return nothing more. All women deserve this. And so do the men in their lives."

Dear God, but she was lost. Her mind argued that he could not mean those words, could not possibly understand what he described. To have respect and tenderness—she could imagine nothing finer.

Except perhaps, to be loved by Jareth.

Her heart seemed to swell and her breath came quickly at the idea. He seemed to sense the change in her, for the blue of his eyes deepened and his hand came to rest on her shoulder in a brief caress. She laid her hand over his.

Applause made him freeze. He pulled away from her as if burned and turned to bow to his audience, who enthusiastically acknowledged him.

Eloise shrank back in her seat. She'd nearly forgotten herself again! Why did she keep tormenting herself with ideas of love and Jareth? The two would never meet, could never be combined. Even if he was reformed, even if he meant those beautiful words, even if he was still attracted to her, it did not follow that he would want to marry her. She would have him no other way.

She lifted her head to find that Mrs. Turner was regarding her thoughtfully from beside a bowing Jareth.

"Remember your own advice, Miss Eloise," she murmured, returning to her seat but keeping her gaze on him. "No dark, enclosed spaces with that one until he proves himself."

"I shall try," Eloise replied with a sigh. "But I have a feeling it will be all too difficult."

Fourteen

As it turned out, it was extremely difficult to put her advice into practice. Jareth remained at Comfort House to answer questions and act out several more scenes. Eloise decided it was the better part of valor to stay in the background, allowing Mrs. Turner to be his partner. His advice generally seemed logical; the few times it strayed into the questionable, the house chaperone chimed in to redirect him.

The sun was setting when they left Comfort House for Eloise's carriage. With her father's coachman on the box and a footman up behind, she had not felt concerned on the drive over. Given the discussion of the afternoon, however, she had doubted that two serving men were enough to protect her from herself. Still, after bringing Jareth here she could hardly insist that he walk home. She squared her shoulders in resolution and led him to the coach.

He was the epitome of a proper gentleman as they took seats opposite each other on the brown velvet upholstered benches and the coachman called to his horses to start. Indeed, Jareth sat so quietly, gaze on the gathering dusk beyond the window glass, that she began to grow concerned.

"Is something the matter, Mr. Darby?" she asked at last.

He met her gaze with a frown. "In truth, I cannot say. Today's efforts have made me pensive, as I suspect you desired."

She cocked her head. "Having second thoughts about your reformation?"

"Indeed, no. Rather the opposite. I find myself wondering whether I have a great deal more for which to atone than I had imagined."

She hid a smile of satisfaction. Had she really made him think about his past actions? If so, her tests were succeeding. Tightening her fingers together in the lap of her calico gown, she cautioned herself not to give in to optimism just yet. As Mrs. Turner had warned, she must judge his motives by his actions.

He did not seem to expect her to disagree with him. Instead, she found him watching her closely again.

"Tell me honestly, Eloise," he said suddenly, "when we met that last time in the hayloft, did I force myself upon you?"

She could not suppress a shudder at the idea. He closed his eyes as if she had struck him.

"Not forced," she assured him hurriedly. "It was not rape, if that's what you ask."

He opened his eyes. "Thank God for that. Given today's discussion, I had begun to wonder. I truly thought you were out for a bit of fun, just as I was."

She shook her head. "I don't think I ever considered our activities 'fun.' Exciting, romantic, a bit terrifying at moments, but never 'fun.' "

"The exciting and romantic part I can certainly understand. Why do you add terrifying?"

She felt her eyes widen. "Did you never stop to consider what would happen if we were caught?"

He quirked a smile. "I never stopped to consider we might be caught."

She shook her head again, this time at his unshakable belief in himself. "But when we were caught, did that not concern you, even a little? You walked away as if there were no need to look back."

She could hear the kindness in his voice as he attempted to tease her away from a painful subject. "I didn't walk, if I recall. I limped."

She wished again that she had his gift for making light of things. "I suspect Cleo, Lady Hastings, was as embarrassed about the situation as you were," she told him. "She came after you because she thought it was force, you see."

He shook his head. "What a mess all around. I suppose we should be pleased that we three were the only ones the wiser."

"Four," she admitted. "Cleo was so certain I had been hurt that she unburdened herself to Miss Martingale."

His smile faded. "The headmistress? How can that be? Had she known, she would have gone straight to the earl. I have little doubt my older brother Adam would have insisted that I do right by you and offer marriage. At the very least, Miss Martingale would have alerted your father. Certainly he would have been out for my blood."

She had long ago thought out all those possibilities. "Oh, never fear. Neither of our families knew of our contretemps then."

He breathed a sigh of what had to be relief. "I had no idea the old girl was willing to listen to you that way."

Eloise sighed as well, but she knew it did not come from relief. "She wasn't. Miss Martingale owes her allegiance to one thing: the name of Darby. When I threatened that, she made sure I was silent."

"What do you mean?" he asked with a frown.

She almost told him that it was none of his affair, but she knew that for a lie. It was more than time that Jareth heard the whole. She took a deep breath and plunged in. "After Cleo chased you off . . ."

"After I wisely withdrew," he amended.

"We argue over semantics, but very well. After you wisely withdrew, I was in no condition to reason with Cleo."

"Why was that?" he interrupted. "Did I hurt you after all?"

She knew he meant physically. "No, but it was a little unnerving being left in dishabille in the stables. Then after I returned to the school, I spent a great deal of time pondering your hasty exit." If he could use words to cushion his conscience, so could she. She did not need to tell him the hours she had cried, the number of times she had slipped away the following day to check the tree where they had met each other so many times.

"Cleo became more concerned that I had been ill used," she continued resolutely, "so she told Miss Martingale everything she had seen. I was summoned to the headmistress' office. I did not

fear she would insist upon our marriage. I had
already learned who Miss Martingale favored."

"Lady Hastings was a pet, I take it."

Eloise shook her head. "Oh, no. *I* was Miss Martingale's pet, her best pupil. I am certain that's
why she reacted so harshly to my fall from grace.
You see, she took your side, Jareth. She said I was
a brazen little tart for leading you on and I deserved any unhappiness I had brought upon myself."

"Eloise," he started, paling.

She rushed on, wanting only to get the confession over with. "She said that if I ever mentioned
the incident to a soul, including my own father,
she would denounce me to the world. She con-
fined me to the sick ward for the remainder of
the term and burned the letters I tried to send
my father. When I was late for my monthly cycle,
she had the doctor purge my body in case I was
carrying something of embarrassment to the great
Darby family."

"You were with child?" His face was as white as
his silk cravat, but she could feel no pain except
her own. Why was this so hard to relive? Had she
not done so dozens of times over the years? Of
course, she had never had an audience before,
especially an audience who had helped precipi-
tate the events.

"I was not with child, thank God," she told
him. "If I had been, I shudder to think what
would have happened—to me or to the babe. As
it was, when I was allowed to return to classes, I
looked ill, which made Miss Martingale's lie seem
the truth. Only Cleo knew otherwise, and she was

too confused by Miss Martingale's story to even speak to me."

"My God," he murmured. "Small wonder you hate me."

"I don't hate you, Jareth." She felt tears coming and blinked them back. "I don't know what I feel anymore. I thought I'd finally put it all behind me and then you appear and expect me to be civil and simply wave my hand as if none of it ever happened and I can't. God help me, but I can't."

The tears came harder. Despite all her efforts, she could not hold them back. He moved to take her in his arms. When she resisted, he shook his head.

"You need this. Pretend I'm someone else."

She pressed her hands against the wall of his chest, holding him away, the gold buttons of his waistcoat biting through her gloves. "Don't you see, that's part of the problem? It would be all too easy for me to pretend you are someone else. You've been nothing like the picture I've painted all these years. I don't know who you are anymore."

He did not attempt to pull her any closer, but even through her tears she could see the sadness on his face. "I am not so hard to know, Eloise. I'm just a man, a man with faults and foibles, imperfect, prideful, but attempting to better himself. I have no wish to cause you pain. Can you not accept that?"

"Then tell me why!" The words were out before she thought better of them. But she knew as soon as she said them that the truth of the matter was what she needed to hear. If she could just understand what had gone wrong, what she had done wrong, perhaps she could hope to find love again.

"Why what, my dear?" he coaxed.

She could not let her courage fail now. "Why did you simply walk away?" she begged. "I know you were wounded, but when you healed, why did you never return for me? I checked our tree. You left no note."

His gaze skittered away from her, as if something beyond the window drew him. "Leaving a note seemed a cold way to speak to you after what we had shared."

She felt her brow rise. "And simply vanishing was better? I had no word from you at all."

"I had my valet ask questions at the school. I thought you were a teacher on staff, not a student. When he relayed that no gossip was circulating among the staff, I assumed you were safe. I feared to contact you again lest your position be compromised."

She could hear the defensiveness in his voice. Her own voice sounded tired to her. "Then, after all, you never loved me."

"Not then." He succeeded in getting his arms around her, as if he too needed to feel her near. "I cared, Eloise, but not, I see now, enough to be the man you expected. I was too green, too spoiled. I listen to you tell me how my actions affected you and I cringe."

She gazed at him in wonder. "Really?"

He smiled as he used his thumb to wipe away her tears. "Really, my sweet." His smile faded, and lines appeared on the sides of his mouth and eyes as if he had suddenly aged. "I was stupid, Eloise.

And in my stupidity, I hurt you badly. Can you ever forgive me?"

"I don't know." She held herself stiff in his arms, resisting the almost overwhelming desire to lean against his strength. She feared that that strength was largely illusionary; it would not be there if she really needed it. "I know it is wrong to hold these feelings against you, Jareth. I begin to believe you are changed. Is it too much to ask that you prove it?"

"It is your right," he said simply. His hand caressed her cheek, his touch gentle. It would be all too easy to read a promise in the sweetness. She fought against the urge.

"I meant what I said at Comfort House," he continued. "You should be with a man who respects and cherishes you, Eloise. I am sorry I was unable to be that man when last we met. Have I lost all right to be that man now?"

She blinked back tears. His face was once again solemn, his eyes deep with emotions she could not name.

"Do you truly wish to be that man?" she challenged. "This time I will settle for nothing less than marriage."

He did not flinch. "Agreed. And yes, I begin to think I do so wish. No woman has ever touched my heart as you do. That hasn't changed. Do you feel anything for me? Could you come to care again?"

She felt herself start to tremble. The truth was she was already coming to care all too much. Unfortunately, her ability to trust him did not seem to be growing apace with her other feelings. "I . . . I don't know," she admitted.

"Perhaps this will help you decide."

He leaned forward to caress her mouth with a kiss. Unlike the hot, urgent kisses she remembered, this touch was a promise of tenderness, of utter devotion. She felt herself sinking into it, drinking him in. He deepened the kiss, gathering her even closer, until her body was cradled by his. Her hands slid up around his neck, stroking hair that was indeed still like satin. She relished the strength of the arms that held her. She wanted to believe, needed to believe, that that strength would be hers forever. That this time, the end of their passion would be a joining, not a dissolution.

He broke off and pulled away from her so suddenly that she gasped aloud. His eyes were deep pools of blue, his face flushed. He let his hand caress her face a moment.

"Jareth?" she asked with a frown.

To her surprise, he reached up and rapped sharply on the roof. "Stop the coach!"

She grabbed his lapel. "What is it?"

"Merely practicing what I preach," he assured her. While the carriage slowed, he pressed a quick kiss on her lips. This one was more insistent, as impulsive as the ones she had once shared with him. He broke off as the footman opened the door.

"Something wrong, sir?" the young man asked with a frown.

"I shall get out here," Jareth explained.

Disappointment stabbed her heart. He was running away from her again.

"Jareth," she began in warning.

Already at the door, he paused to glance back at her. "You are magnificent," he pronounced, stopping whatever else she had been about to say. His smile changed from appreciation to teasing once more.

"Remember," he advised, "dark, enclosed spaces tend to send my mind in inappropriate directions. And as I am a reformed rake, I shall leave you before I am tempted further. Let me know when you wish to begin the last test, my dear Eloise."

He was honoring her wishes, above his own desires. Her heart swelled, but he was gone before she could tell him he may just have passed the only test that mattered.

Fifteen

Jareth returned to his room that night with a great deal on his mind. He finally understood what Eloise held against him. He could not change the past, but he could change the present. He would not wait until she told him what the final test would be. He had a renewed opportunity to persuade her. The question had become what exactly he wanted to persuade her to do.

Certainly he still needed her forgiveness. Only that day, Justinian had received a note from the local pastor of the church nearest the estate at Cheddar Cliffs. The estate manager had been relieved of his duties because of poor health. A new replacement was needed immediately. If Jareth didn't follow through on his promise, he could very well lose the position entirely.

Yet his interest in Eloise had progressed beyond the desire for the estate. He meant every word he had said in the coach that day. Marriage, particularly marriage to Eloise, did not look so undesirable. Unfortunately, particularly given their last conversation, he knew how hard he would have to work to prove to her that he was worthy of her forgiveness.

He started by sending her flowers. Of course,

he had to negotiate with a fellow who owned a greenhouse out in Kensington, but after tutoring the man's two sons in fisticuffs, he was able to procure five dozen roses for Eloise, one dozen for each year since they had parted. The bruises he endured were worth it, for the flowers were prominently displayed when next he called. Eloise's reception of him was also beyond the polite, which gave him hope that he might be succeeding.

Indeed, it appeared that her attitude toward him had changed as well. Not only did she readily accept his invitation to dance when they attended the same balls in the days that followed, but she let him call upon her, take her driving, join her on visits to friends.

But as he went about living the life of a proper English gentleman with her, he began to see additional changes, in himself. His old pastimes had lost their luster. Gaming amidst the stale stench of cigars and old Madeira was not nearly as heady as inhaling the scent of Eloise's hair as she leaned close to him at the theatre. The excitement of holding the reins of his brother's curricle for a race could not compare to the thrill of holding Eloise in his arms, however fleetingly, on the dance floor. Telling her about his future hopes was infinitely more satisfying than contemplating those dreams alone.

She had seemed surprised by his desire to become the master of Cheddar Cliffs. "I have not known you to rusticate," she told him after one of their discussions of the place.

"I cannot see it as rustication," he assured her, "but living well. Hunting, fishing, living off the fruits of your lands, your loved ones gathered round you."

The picture was easy to paint. And it did not surprise him that the mother in the center of that picture bore a striking resemblance to the woman seated beside him. He was clearly on the road to reformation.

Other people noticed the change in him. Mothers of eligible young ladies, though still watchful, were more likely to allow their daughters to dance with him. Portly older gentlemen who once had grunted gruffly or turned their backs on him now were willing to engage him in conversation. If he happened to air an opinion before the members of Parliament with whom his brother associated, they listened.

Only Portia Sinclair went out of her way to attract him. She and her stepmother could be found at nearly every event he attended. Still, even Portia was more likely to smile at him from across the room rather than approach him directly.

That changed the night of his brother's literary reading.

Years before the scandal, Justinian had confided in him his interest in becoming a novelist. Although Jareth had encouraged him then, it had taken Eleanor to find a way for his brother to feel comfortable publishing his work. His three novels so far had been issued anonymously, but to some acclaim.

Justinian delighted in using his position to bring new writers into fashion. But, if tonight's event was any indication, his brother had his work cut out for him. Jareth had to keep pinching himself to remain awake as the author droned on about his home in the heathery hills of Hampstead.

It did not help that Eloise had declined the invitation he had insisted Eleanor send. Since their conversation on the way home from Comfort House, they had had little time alone. He knew any number of locations in the Darby townhouse where they could seclude themselves without anyone being the wiser. The desire was contrary to his reformed image, but he didn't much care. Being with Eloise made him feel good. He had been a perfect gentleman of late, and he was hoping he might convince her to let him be just the tiniest bit bad.

But she could not attend, claiming a theatre engagement with her father. To make matters worse, the Hastingses did attend. He had asked Eleanor to invite them as well, thinking that their presence would please Eloise. As it was, he had to endure Lady Hastings's censorious frown for much of the evening.

The only person who seemed pleased to see him was Portia Sinclair. She obviously saw the fact that he was alone as an open invitation. She and her stepmother took two chairs beside him and the girl spent much of the reading finding excuses to lean her body against his. At any moment, he was never certain whether he'd find some bit of her gauzy white gown draped over the blue velvet of his coat and knee breeches.

At first it had been mildly flattering. Within a half hour, it was tedious. By intermission, it was embarrassing. Several of the other attendees had obviously noticed, as he saw the number of frowning glances in his direction increasing. It didn't help that the room boasted large, gilt-framed mirrors at one end that seemed to magnify everything Portia did. Even Portia's stepmother began to fidget as if nervous.

The matter equally annoyed his sister-in-law. She sought him out as soon as her guests had been directed toward the refreshment buffet next door in the forward salon.

"I have had to swear to your reformation to no less than five august personages," Eleanor murmured, taking his arm with one hand and drawing aside her gray satin skirts with the other for a promenade about the nearly empty room. "Do you intend to make me a liar in my own house, sir?"

"Not in the slightest," Jareth promised her, being careful to avoid eye contact with Portia, who was hovering near the door. "But the chit persists in clinging. Short of a firing squad, I cannot find a way to rid myself of her."

"This is a literary event, not a military encampment, sir."

"What would you have me do? Declaim her to death?"

She tapped his arm lightly with her ebony fan, but her eyes twinkled. "Fie, sir. I expect better of the infamous Jareth Darby."

"Ah, but I thought you wished me to forego the pleasures of my infamous nature. Tell me, madam, how can I politely tell the girl she is hunting the wrong fox?"

He had been so intent on the conversation that when Eleanor stopped with a frown, he thought it must be in consideration of her answer. Instead, a clear voice piped up. "Lady Wenworth, for shame! How can you be so cruel as to monopolize the most eligible bachelor here?"

Jareth grit his teeth, but kept a polite smile in place at the sight of Miss Sinclair effectively blocking their way across the expanse of blue and yellow carpet. Her gloved hands were on the hips of her puffed-sleeve gown, her color nearly as high as the rosy ribbons that bordered the low neckline.

"Why, I do believe my brother-in-law understands monopolization," Eleanor replied, smiling coolly at him. "Just look at how utterly devoted he is to the fair Miss Watkin. What a shame she could not attend tonight."

"A decided shame," Portia said cheerfully. "It remains for the rest of us present to console him on her absence."

"She is not dead, Miss Sinclair," Eleanor pointed out, snapping open her fan as if intent on blowing the girl away, "merely unavailable. I daresay Mr. Darby will survive."

Jareth extracted his arm from hers. "Actually, I find myself completely lost without her. To keep your party from becoming as depressed as I am, dear lady, I shall withdraw. Goodnight, Sister Eleanor, Miss Sinclair."

He strode away from them, congratulating himself on a neat escape, from both the reading and the daring Miss Sinclair. On his way out, he bade farewell to some acquaintances as well as the fledgling author. He had not reached the stairs before a sharp hiss stopped him. Portia's stepmother, a dark cloud in her gown of matte brown satin, materialized out of the archway that led to the servant's stair. "Mr. Darby, a word with you."

He paused, inclining his head. "Your servant, madam."

"I must ask," she hurried on, her gaze darting about as if she expected the portraits on the soft white walls to censure her, "what are your intentions toward my stepdaughter?"

"I have no intentions, madam," he told her frankly. "Now, if you will excuse me."

As he put a foot on the stair, she seized his arm with fingers that bit into his flesh through the velvet coat. "No, wait, please. There are circumstances you cannot know."

Jareth paused to regard her. Tears welled in her eyes. Once before he had stopped to help a lady in distress. The results had not been good. Still, he was supposed to be more a gentleman now than he had been then. "What do you mean?" he asked cautiously.

She swallowed, blinking back her tears. "I dare not tell you here."

Jareth frowned. "We are alone. What do you fear?"

"We could be interrupted at any moment." As if to confirm her, laughter bubbled out of the open door to the forward salon. She wiped hastily at her cheeks, and Jareth pulled a handkerchief from his pocket to aid her. She smiled as she took it, but the look held more triumph than gratitude.

"There is a small sitting room just down the corridor, is there not?" she ventured. "Can we go there?"

Jareth hesitated. He could feel her fear, but not

sense its cause. It might well be connected with the dire secret she wished to impart, but it could also be connected to another purpose. Unfortunately, the only way to find out was to go with her. Reluctantly, he bowed her in front of him.

She hurried across the corridor, her movements as agitated as her conversation. But when she reached the sitting room, she motioned to him to precede her into the ill-lit room. Jareth stepped through the open door and heard it snap shut behind him. He whirled, but a voice in the darkened room stayed him.

"Forgive the subterfuge, Mr. Darby. My stepmother said it was the only way to get you alone."

Jareth turned to gaze into the room. Lit only by the glow of a dying fire, the pastel furniture looked rosy red, as did the face and figure of Portia Sinclair.

"You expect me to believe your stepmother approves of this?" he demanded.

She took a step toward him, gown whispering. "Most certainly. She suggested it would be seemly for me to explain that many people believe you have already compromised me and beg you to see the error of your ways."

Jareth leaned against the door and crossed his arms over his chest. "What game are you playing, Miss Sinclair? I've never compromised you. In fact, you know very well my behavior has been above reproach."

She hurried to close the distance between them. He could see the eagerness in her smile. "But your politeness has been against your desire, has it not? I have seen the light in your eyes. You are intrigued with me."

"Perhaps at one time," he allowed. "I will own you were a temptation at first. But sadly, Miss Sinclair, I am truly reformed. You will have to find yourself another playmate."

"But I don't want another playmate." Her smile faded. "I must have you."

"I should be flattered, but my interests lie elsewhere."

She frowned for a moment, then evidently decided to try again. Reaching up, she pulled the pins from her soft red-gold hair, shaking her head to let her tresses fall about her shoulders. "You don't need to look elsewhere. I can satisfy your needs, Jareth. I can make you happy. Let me show you."

She slipped her arms about his neck and pressed herself against him as her lips sought his. Jareth felt a curious detachment. The softness of her body touched him, and it raised no excitement. He smelled the sweetness of her hair and found it cloying. He tasted the caress of her kiss, and it brought only annoyance.

She stepped away from him with a frown as if she realized his lack of response. "You are not pleased. Should I try again?"

"No, Miss Sinclair," Jareth replied quellingly. "I am not interested. Peddle your wares elsewhere. I am reformed." He started to turn away, but heard her sigh.

"I am very sorry, Mr. Darby. Please believe me. I hope you'll understand someday. It is simply too late for me to go elsewhere."

Her words implied some dire secret. He turned back. She had seated herself on the biggest chair in the room. Slowly, she raised the hem of her skirt, baring her ankles, her calves, her knees. Jareth shook his head, turning his back on her.

"Miss Sinclair," he said as he reached for the door handle, "I wish you would believe me. I have no need for a further demonstration of your ardor."

At the level of his chest, someone tapped softly at the door. He stiffened.

"This display isn't for you, Mr. Darby," Portia said sadly behind him. She raised her voice to a high pitch of alarm. "Oh, stop, Jareth my darling. What if we are discovered?"

The door opened as if on cue, and he found himself looking down at Mrs. Sinclair on the threshold. Her flabby face was white, her large hands worrying before her. She was the epitome of the concerned mother, except that her eyes were clear and calculating. She did not meet his gaze, her own going immediately to her stepdaughter beyond.

"Is it done?" she demanded.

"Yes," Portia whispered.

"On the contrary," Jareth said coldly, realizing Mrs. Sinclair was indeed the instigator of Portia's plan. "You are undone, madam. I leave you to minister to your stepdaughter."

He half expected the woman to reach out to stop him, but she did not move a finger. When he pushed past her, he realized she had no need. The sight beyond her was quite enough.

Eleanor stood with Lord and Lady Hastings and several other guests in the corridor. Lord Hastings was frowning, dark brows drawn tightly over his long nose, his look nearly as black as the evening clothes he wore. Lady Hastings's mouth hung nearly to the bosom of her lacy saffron gown, as if she could not catch her breath in amazement at his audacity. Around them, the other guests stood with looks of equal surprise.

Eleanor's face was as white as Mrs. Sinclair's. She met his gaze with eyes wide in shock. He wished he could think of a single clever thing to say, some charming trick to wipe away her embarrassment, but for once in his life, nothing came to mind. Perhaps because, he realized, for once in his life, he was innocent.

The irony was exquisite. He threw back his head and laughed. The guests recoiled, cast each other worried glances, began to murmur. The murmurs only increased when Portia appeared in the doorway, leaning heavily on her stepmother's arm and pulling furtively at her gown as if she had been through a great deal.

Her gray eyes widened as if she were shocked to find so many people witness to her supposed fall.

"Mr. Darby?" she murmured pathetically, reaching out a hand to him. "You would not abandon me?"

He glanced at her, then back at Eleanor and the others. Lady Hastings's face was a thundercloud. He was doomed.

"Cheerfully, Miss Sinclair," he said in ringing tones. "After all, isn't that what everyone would expect from the infamous Jareth Darby?"

Sixteen

Eloise had not even finished her solitary breakfast the following morning before she learned of the night's events. She had spent a lovely evening at the theatre with her father, one of the few times he had deigned to take her out. His conversation had been pleasant and the Shakespearean drama well acted. The only thing that marred her enjoyment of the evening was the fact that she missed Jareth.

Even that morning she marveled at it as she dressed in a cambric gown trimmed with lace. She would never have imagined that she would find herself missing him again. Yet as she finished her oat muffin, she had to own that she was greatly hoping he would call that afternoon.

She certainly didn't expect to see him so early, or to see Cleo. She nearly dropped her cup of cocoa when the breakfast room door burst open and her friend stalked into the room. Bryerton, at her heels, was as composed as ever, but Eloise thought his color seemed just a bit pink, as if he had run to keep up with the young marchioness.

"Lady Hastings to see you, Miss Watkin," he said, even as Cleo blurted, "He's a fraud!" Then she glanced pointedly at the butler, who had the good sense to bow and withdraw.

"Since you cannot mean Bryerton," Eloise said, motioning her friend to a seat, "I assume you mean Jareth Darby."

Cleo pulled out the chair beside Eloise and threw herself into it with such vehemence that she rumpled the skirts of her striped silk walking dress. "Of course I mean Jareth Darby. You have every right to cut him off, Eloise. He has not changed in the slightest."

Eloise waited for her stomach to clench or her heart to slow in disappointment, but nothing happened. It was as if her emotions had shut down now that her original thoughts might prove true. She pushed her cocoa away. "What's happened?"

Cleo was obviously too upset to notice her muted response. "He was caught last night trying to seduce Portia Sinclair. I was there; I saw him. And in his own brother's house, no less!"

Eloise's gaze focused on a red spot on the white figured-damask tablecloth. She could not imagine how the stain had gotten there. She rubbed at it absently with her thumb. "It seems odd he would attempt seduction," she pointed out to Cleo, "knowing you were watching."

"Of course he didn't do so before my eyes," Cleo informed her testily. "We had reached an interval in the program. Most of us had gone into another room for refreshments. Mr. Darby had excused himself, claiming of all things that he could not enjoy the evening without you there."

Eloise felt a smile curving her lips. So, he had missed her as well. Shouldn't that make it even less likely that he would seduce another woman? She rubbed a little harder on the red spot.

"Eloise, this is nothing to smile about," Cleo insisted. "His claim was no more than a humbug. Shortly after he left, Miss Sinclair and her step-mother left us as well, I assumed to visit the ladies' retiring room. The next thing anyone knew, Mrs. Sinclair was looking for Portia, only to find her barely clothed in a dark sitting room with Jareth."

The spot only grew wider. Eloise licked her thumb and reapplied it. "And you are certain she did not entrap him?"

"One doesn't need to trap a hand-fed fox," Cleo retorted.

Eloise nodded. The damask tore under her thumbnail; she frowned at the polished walnut showing through.

Cleo's hand came down to still hers. "Eloise, what is wrong with you? I tell you our suspicions about Jareth Darby are correct and you sit with less animation than if I had asked your opinion of a new bonnet. Why do you not cry foul?"

She wasn't sure. It was as if her heart was co-cooned in soft fabric, muffled, hidden. The only hint of feeling was a deep need to be in Jareth's arms.

"Perhaps I would like to hear it from his lips," she said.

"And so you shall," Jareth announced from the doorway.

Eloise's head jerked up. The sight of him tore through the cover on her heart, like sun burning away a morning mist.

"Mr. Darby to see you, Miss Watkin," Bryerton

mumbled behind him. "I informed him you had a visitor, but he refused to wait."

Her butler's face was impassive, but he seemed even more flustered. She nodded to him.

"It's all right, Bryerton. I'm sure you did your best. You may go."

She thought she heard a sigh as her servant exited.

Jareth remained standing near the door. His color was as high as the butler's, and she could not help noticing that he looked as if he had thrown his clothes on his lean body. His cravat was barely knotted, his embroidered vest was buttoned crookedly, and his navy coat clashed with the blue velvet knee breeches he wore.

"Forgive the interruption," he said, "but I wanted you to hear the tale first from me. I should have guessed Lady Hastings would be equally fervent to carry the news to you."

Cleo glared at him. "You are quite right that she deserved to hear it from a friend."

"I should think the truth to be preferable to gossip, whatever the source," he countered.

"And as you seem incapable of stating the truth, you can see why I thought I would be needed."

Eloise wanted only to close the distance between her and Jareth. She held up her hand to forestall any further comments from her friend.

"What would you tell me, Mr. Darby?" she asked. "Are you innocent of this allegation of seduction?"

"Completely," he said, moving around the table to sit opposite Cleo, and keeping Eloise's gaze as he did so. "Believe me, the fact surprises me as much as it must you."

"How can you lie so egregiously?" Cleo demanded. "You were caught in the act!"

Eloise's heart, now freed, jerked painfully.

"I was found," he countered with a flash of his eyes, "in a room alone with Portia Sinclair. I am guilty of nothing more than being stupid enough to listen to a woman's story."

"No more stupid than a woman to listen to a man's," Eloise murmured. He flinched but she took no pleasure in it. "So, you would have me believe she led you on? Played with your heart?"

"My heart was not involved," Jareth began, but Cleo interrupted.

"Now *that* I believe. I am not certain you possess a heart."

Jareth shook his head, but Eloise took a deep breath to steady herself and turned to her outraged friend. "Cleo, I understand what you are feeling. You know that to be true. But I believe this is a matter between Mr. Darby and me."

"How can you say that?" Cleo protested. "I cannot sit by and watch you throw your life away. I did not help you before. I won't leave you alone again."

Eloise reached out to squeeze her hand. "You are not abandoning me, Cleo. There are simply some things I must do for myself."

Cleo gazed at her a moment longer, dark eyes stormy, then nodded. With a last glare at Jareth, she rose and left them.

Eloise turned to him to find him frowning.

"She blames herself for that incident in the

loft," he said, as if making a great discovery. "That's why she hates me."

"In her eyes, your actions were despicable," Eloise replied. "You were quite the villain, at least in those days."

He sighed. "I am getting heartily tired of confessing that I have changed. But it is the truth, Eloise. I am innocent of this."

She smiled sadly. "You'll never be completely innocent, Jareth. You have too much of a past."

His mouth tightened. "Then you blame me for this as well?"

She shook her head, feeling her fingers clench in the damask. A determination was forming inside her. Having Jareth as her suitor had given her more cause to hope for her future than ever before. She refused to abandon that hope so easily.

"No, I do not place blame," she told him. "Trust has to start somewhere. If you tell me you are innocent, then I must believe you."

He eyed her for a moment, head cocked, then straightened and nodded as if he believed her as well. "Thank you for that. You cannot know what it means to me that you would offer your trust, particularly under these circumstances. I promise you, this time I will not betray you."

"I shall hold you to that promise," she threatened.

He took her hand and raised it to his lips, pressing a kiss against her bare knuckles that set her heart to pounding anew. "You must do more than hold me to a promise, Eloise. You must hold me to your heart."

She gazed at his solemn face. "Is that truly what you want, Jareth?"

"It is. Is that not what you ask of me?"

Was it? Was that what she truly wanted, that Jareth would fall in love with her and want only to hold her close? Revenge had indeed paled, but she was still unsure as to what emotion had taken its place. "In truth, I do not know what to ask of you. And if it were love, could you give it?"

He kissed her hand again, lingering over the caress. It was only a short distance to raise his head and meet her lips. Though his kiss was gentle, she felt desire building inside her.

When he moved away, his gaze was dark with emotion. "For you, yes, I could give my love, and gladly. I barely slept last night thinking how you would react when the gossip reached you. I have never felt so afraid."

"You, afraid? You have escaped censure too many times to dread it now."

"It wasn't censure that I feared," he assured her. "I could not stand the thought of losing you."

His words were exactly what her heart needed to hear. Why did her brain keep protesting that she should not believe him?

"I was a fool to walk away before," he continued. "You will not rid yourself of me so easily this time."

"I pray that is true, Jareth," she managed. "Now you had better go. I must smooth Cleo's feathers."

He kept her hand. "Not until you tell me when I may see you again."

She shook her head at his tone. This was the

spoiled Jareth she remembered. Still, if he was true in his devotion, she should not punish him by absenting herself. "Tonight. I have vouchers for Almack's."

He squeezed her hand. "Then I shall see you at Almack's." Rising, he bowed. She inclined her head and watched him stride from the room.

Given her emotional state that morning, she half expected her determination to leave with him. Yet it only seemed to grow as she went in search of Cleo. It took some effort to convince her friend that she did not intend to repeat the mistakes of her past. But the more Cleo protested, the firmer grew Eloise's resolve. With it grew her conviction of Jareth's innocence.

It was no different at Almack's that evening. The gossip about the event spread from one knot of people to another as if blown by the wind of fluttering fans. She heard three versions of the story before she reached the dance floor with Lord Nathaniel, who had begged to be her first partner. In all versions, Jareth was the villain.

"You seem quiet tonight, Miss Watkin," the young viscount observed as they stood out in the dance. "I hope this pernicious gossip does not distress you."

"It has nothing to do with me, my lord," she replied calmly. Her gaze continued roaming the room, searching for a tall, platinum-haired gentleman. Until she knew he was here, she could not relax. She was a little surprised Lord Nathaniel saw her as calm.

"How very glad I am to hear that you are not concerned," Nathaniel continued. "I had begun to fear Mr. Darby had ensnared you in his web as well."

Jareth entered Almack's, and the evening changed. The very air seemed to sparkle with a new clarity. He wore his deep blue velvet, but somehow she thought he stood taller, filled the double-breasted coat more fully. He quite eclipsed poor Lord Nathaniel in his durable brown coat and breeches. She took a deep breath. "Oh, no, my lord," she assured the viscount as they took hands to return to the dance, "I would not allow myself to be ensnared so easily."

"Not even by me?" he asked tentatively.

Eloise smiled. "Ah, but you have better sense than to make an offer for me, my lord. Haven't you proved that time and again?"

He looked as if he would argue with her, but the dance ended and Jareth stepped to her side.

Lord Nathaniel frowned, but bowed. "Mr. Darby, I am surprised to see you here."

Jareth returned his bow. "With every lovely lady in London under this roof, where else would I be?"

"Posting for the Continent?" Lord Nathaniel suggested, but when Jareth coldly raised a brow, he hastily amended. "I understand you are sorely missed there."

"Alas, I sincerely doubt that," Jareth replied. "My talents are rarely appreciated, unlike Miss Watkin's. I vow you hold every eye in the room, madam."

Eloise felt herself dimple. "You are too kind, sir."

"Ah, but Mr. Darby is correct, Miss Watkin,"

Lord Nathaniel put in. "No lady can hold a candle to you."

"You will turn my head with your compliments, my lord. Besides, if I possess any skills in the dance, they are a result of my partner." She smiled kindly into his boyish face.

"Nonsense, Miss Watkin," Jareth protested as Lord Nathaniel colored with obvious pleasure. "You make even his lordship here look gallant. May I request that you do the same for me?"

"I believe," Lord Nathaniel said firmly, "that Miss Watkin had expressed a desire to sit out this next set. Is that not so, my dear?"

His hand was on her elbow. Lord Nathaniel, turning possessive? A shame he had waited so long to decide he wanted her. But then, he had never stood a chance against her feelings for Jareth. She stepped away from him even as the music started. "You must have misunderstood me, my lord. I can certainly spare Mr. Darby a dance."

Jareth's smile was welcoming as he swept her into his arms and out onto the floor.

Of course it had to be a waltz. So close, she was all the more aware of the blue of his gaze, the sweet curve of his lips, and power in the arms that held her.

"He was right to try to keep you away from me, Eloise," Jareth murmured after they had danced in silence for a time. "I am beginning to see that I have never been worthy of you."

"Such humility, Mr. Darby," she teased. "Be careful or I shall begin to believe you all too reformed."

"I have yet to pass your third test," he reminded her. "What more proof can I give you?"

"I have yet to decide."

"What, madam, has that fertile mind of yours at last run out of ways to humble me? Perhaps I should speak to your father."

She knew him too well to think him serious. "La, Mr. Darby," she said with a laugh, "why would you do such a thing? What will people say?"

His gaze darkened. "I care nothing for what people say. The only opinion that matters is yours, Eloise."

When she gazed up at him, surprised, he continued. "I was only half in jest just now. With your permission, I should like to call on your father."

Seventeen

She actually halted, staring at him while the other couples maneuvered around them with frowns of annoyance or wide-eyed looks of curiosity. Jareth used the excuse to bring her closer, hand and hip encouraging her to continue waltzing with him. As always, the touch of her body against his was sweet. She must have felt it as well, for she pulled herself back to a reasonable distance.

"Have I truly stunned you?" he asked quietly as they moved together. "Surely you know my feelings for you."

"I am certain I could not begin to fathom your feelings, Mr. Darby," she replied. He could feel her resistance, the way she leaned back to keep herself as far from him as possible. Indeed, his arms were stretched to maintain a hand on her back.

"I have been rather pointed in my attentions," he reminded her gently. "But if you like, I can say the pretty words. I am a little surprised you would want them said here, in front of all Almack's."

She shook her head. "Surely you know by now that words will not sway me."

Now it was his turn to hesitate. Luckily, the dance was ending and he was able to turn the gaff into a bow of sorts. "Then I have lost? You refuse forgiveness?"

"Forgiveness?" She stepped further away from him, but her face was a study of sadness. "Is that all you ask of me?"

"No, I want your love."

Her eyes widened, but Jareth was all too aware of other eyes. The two of them were the objects of every stare in the room. He bowed again. "We cannot talk here. May I see you home?"

"In a dark, enclosed space?" She shook her head. "No indeed. I learn some lessons well, my lord."

He blew out his breath in frustration. "Help me, Eloise. I don't know how to reach you."

She glanced about as if realizing the gossip they were causing. "It is late, but the night is warm. Perhaps you could walk me down the street to meet my carriage."

Though that was an equal violation of the rules he had laid down at Comfort House, he knew better than to argue. He nodded and escorted her to get her things.

Lady Hastings neatly intercepted them. Her head was high, her bearing militant. Before she could even open her mouth, however, Eloise held up a hand.

"No more, Cleo," she ordered. "Mr. Darby is going to see me out. I assure you I am the master of my emotions."

Something in Eloise's eyes must have assured her, for the little marchioness nodded. "Let me only walk you to the door for propriety's sake."

Eloise agreed. Jareth could not argue, but he felt the marchioness' gaze on him all the way down the stairs to the street.

Outside, Eloise took Jareth's arm to start up the street, following the line of waiting carriages. Normally her coachman would have come at her call, but Jareth knew she was giving him a few moments to speak with her alone. The night was warm, but the smells of a humid city in summer were hardly conducive to romance. The night seemed to be conducive to little else either, for other than the carriages and attendants the street was nearly deserted in all directions. Beside him, Eloise was no more welcoming than their surroundings. The only sound was the swish of her skirts, the creak of the carriages, and the uneasy shuffling of horses' hooves.

"I somehow had another image of the moment in which I would propose to you," Jareth said. "But I'm game if you are."

"There is no need to propose to me," Eloise replied. "I did not make that a condition to prove your reformation."

"Nor is it one," Jareth assured her. "I wish to offer, Eloise. I love you."

She sucked in a breath. "Really?"

He turned to look at her and met the longing in those green eyes. "Really, truly, madly. I am utterly devoted. But that should come as no surprise. You are intelligent, charming, beautiful, and caring. It is not surprising that I fell in love. Only that I did not fall sooner."

She looked away as if she still could not bring herself to believe him. "Perhaps it is only your desire to settle down that motivates you," she maintained, pace steady. "Knowing me years ago makes you think you could love me."

He frowned. "Why do you seek to argue it away? I was under the impression you would welcome my suit."

She stiffened. "Do I appear so desperate?"

"Must you be desperate to love me?" he countered.

When she bit her lip, he sighed. "Forgive me, Eloise. Once more I seem to have done you a disservice. I appear to be incapable of understanding you. Let me walk you to your coach."

A bitter laugh bubbled up. "So, once again, Mr. Darby gives up."

"Is this your third test, then?" he demanded. "Am I to persevere through whatever barriers you erect?"

"And if I said yes, would you?"

"If I knew that, in the end, I would win your heart—gladly. But something tells me you hold your heart deeply. Has nothing I've done proved to you that my intentions toward you are honorable this time?"

He wasn't sure she would answer the question. Indeed, she was silent for a few moments as if considering it herself. "You want to speak to my father," she finally said. "That in itself tells me you are serious. And I find that thought suddenly terrifying."

"Why?"

She scowled. "Because you can hurt me again, Jareth, more deeply and fully than ever you could before."

"I promise you I have no desire to hurt you again. I never wanted to hurt you the first time."

"Yet you did. I don't know if I have the courage to give you that power over me again."

"So you would settle for a passionless marriage to Lord Nathaniel rather than what we might share?"

As soon as he spoke he knew he should have been silent. Her feelings for Lord Nathaniel or lack thereof had no purpose in this discussion.

She rounded on him, as he had expected. "Leave Lord Nathaniel out of this."

"I would," he replied, "but it strikes me that he is an example of how you have tried to put up a wall between us. Have you not noticed that you chose to encourage a gentleman who is my exact opposite?"

She raised a brow. "Because he is reliable and stable, do you mean?"

Much as he would have liked to argue, he couldn't. "Oh, I will grant you I am far less stable than his lordship. With Lord Nathaniel, you need never fear that your husband would surprise you in the garden and sweep you off into a bower to kiss you senseless. You can rest assured he will not bring you your favorite flower simply because it pleases him. Indeed, he will likely not remember your favorite flower or even think to ask."

"Do you remember?" she challenged.

"Certainly I remember. I remember the day we walked in the fields behind the manor and you told me all about yourself. Your favorite color is purple, your favorite food a cinnamon apple crumble only your father's cook can make, and your favorite flowers are painted daisies, in armfuls of red, orange, and pink."

She shook her head in what he hoped was reluctant admiration. "You're right. I cannot imagine how you remembered all that."

He stopped her. "I remember many things about you, Eloise. The way your hair smells like lilacs. The way your laugh rises and falls like a brook in a spring freshet. The way your body feels like . . ."

"That is enough," she said hurriedly, and even in the dim light he could see she was blushing. "You have proven your memory is exceptional."

"And yours is selective. You remember how much I hurt you. Do you remember how much I cared about you? Perhaps I should remind you."

They had reached the familiar coach, but ignoring the coachman just ahead and heedless of what any passersby might think, Jareth gathered Eloise in his arms. Though a part of him demanded that he claim what he knew to be his, he kept the kiss gentle. With his hands and his lips, he coaxed her into remembering how good they could be together, how right it felt to touch and be touched. She was stiff for a moment, then he felt her melting, giving as much as he gave, warming his heart as well as his body.

A deep cough interrupted him and he raised his head to eye the servants in front of them. In the light from the lanterns on either side of the coach, the coachman's frown was almost apologetic.

"Do you need my assistance, Miss Watkin?" he asked gruffly.

Eloise seemed to recall herself as well. "No, thank you, Mr. Butters. Mr. Darby was just saying goodbye."

She was dismissing him, but he felt cause for

hope. Jareth bowed. "As you will, madam. But only for tonight. We have much to discuss."

"Perhaps we do," she allowed. She turned to the coach, and he opened the door and helped her in. Shutting the door, he waved the coachman on. He stood on the pavement until the sound of hooves faded in the distance.

She had built a wall around herself. It had never been clearer to him than tonight. He had to find a way to break through. Third test or not, he fully intended to win her heart.

As he walked to White's, he marveled at his determination. He had planned many a campaign to win a lady, but never had it been her heart he sought. Indeed, he prided himself on leaving hearts alone, his and theirs. Of course, that same pride had more than once been his undoing.

Because of it, he saw now, he had walked away from Eloise once. Because of it, he had fled to the Continent rather than face the stories being told of him and Lady Hendricks. Pride even now kept him from living under his brother's roof. Surely it was a sign of how much he loved Eloise that this pride did not motivate him in seeking her hand.

He smiled to himself. Justinian was right. Love was no match for the cursed Darby pride. A shame he could not have learned that earlier.

The next morning found him at the Watkin townhouse. He had to tell the butler his intentions twice before the fellow consented to take his card in to Lord Watkin. It was only retribution, he supposed, for the way he had shoved past the fellow in his hurry to reach Eloise the day before. Jareth cooled his heels for ten long minutes before the butler returned to escort him to his lordship's richly paneled private study.

As Jareth entered, he was struck again by how little Eloise resembled her father. Where she was a sculptor's ideal of curves, Lord Watkin was built on thin, spare lines. Where she dressed in the latest state of fashion and in shades that suited her dramatic coloring, he chose a plain suit of brown several shades darker than his thinning hair. Where she was tall for a woman, he was short for a man. Her green eyes glowed with warmth; his blue eyes were cool and calculating. The only feature they seemed to share was their alabaster skin. He found it far more charming on Eloise.

Lord Watkin returned his bow and motioned him to a chair before the polished wood desk. "Mr. Darby, a pleasure to meet you," he said in a calm, quiet voice. "How might I be of assistance?"

"In truth it is not your assistance I need," Jareth replied. He had thought to move more slowly to the topic, but the formality of the room and the gentleman before him seemed to brook no roundaboutation. He squared his shoulders. "I would like your permission to ask your daughter for her hand in marriage. But I suspect you will not give it to me."

Lord Watkin raised a thin brow as if mildly intrigued. "And why would I refuse, Mr. Darby? Are you a fortune hunter?"

Jareth laughed. "By no means. I hope soon to have an estate of my own in Somerset. You will have heard of my father and brother, the Earl of Wenworth?"

"Of course. *Those* Darbys. Let me see. The oldest son died in Naples a few years ago. Your older brother Justinian is the current earl, I believe. The young major married some time ago. That would make you . . ."

"The black sheep of the family," Jareth supplied readily. "I have only recently returned from exile on the Continent. But I promise you I have put all that behind me. I can have my family vouch for me if you like. However, I feel it only fair to admit that I was the man who seduced Eloise in school."

There, he had said it. He waited for the explosion. The baron merely eyed him with a slight frown.

"I am afraid, Mr. Darby," he said, "that someone has played a joke on you. My daughter left school several years ago and she was never troubled there. I am certain she would have told me if that were the case."

Jareth stared at him. "Eloise never mentioned the matter to you?"

His frown deepened. "My daughter's name is Eloise, that is true. But she never mentioned any difficulties with boys, and neither did her headmistress."

Jareth's mind reeled. Eloise had claimed that only a few knew of their liaison, but he had assumed she'd eventually told her father. "Forgive me, Lord Watkin. I don't know what to say. I can only encourage you to speak to your daughter about the matter. I know it has caused her some distress, and for that I am gravely sorry. For now,

I can only repeat my request that you allow me to ask her hand in marriage."

"You put me in a difficult position, Mr. Darby." He tapped his chin with his finger. "You tell me you are a reformed scoundrel, yet you wish me to give you complete access to my greatest treasure, Eloise. Even if I believe you are a gentleman now, I cannot feel comfortable with your offer."

"I understand. You are within your right to refuse me. May I point out in my own defense that if I were still a scoundrel, I would have ensured beforehand that your daughter was in a position in which she could not refuse me."

His brow went higher. "And you think it noble you have not done so?"

"No, not noble. Merely an indication that I now try to follow the proper way of doing things."

He pursed his thin lips. "If I were to agree, Mr. Darby, what do you think your chances are of gaining my daughter's acceptance?"

"In the short term, miserable," Jareth admitted. "But I hope to prove to her that I am utterly devoted. I want to be the man to make her happy. If, however, I find I cannot be that man, I will step aside."

Lord Watkin regarded him. Jareth held his breath. Abruptly, Eloise's father nodded. "Very well. You have my permission to pay your respects to my daughter. But I expect to be kept apprised of your progress."

Jareth breathed in relief. "Of course, my lord. Thank you. I will give you no cause to regret this decision."

"See that you do not. Now, I would be delighted to call Eloise for you, but I believe Bryerton told me she is out."

"I made certain she was away before calling on you," Jareth confirmed. "I was uncertain of my reception and did not wish to trouble her. But you can be assured I shall return later, ring in hand, with your permission, of course."

"Granted. Good luck, Mr. Darby."

He grinned. "Thank you, my lord. I have a feeling I shall need it."

Eighteen

Eloise had barely returned from her shopping that morning when Bryerton announced that her father wished to see her. She stiffened in the act of allowing the footman to remove her pelisse. "Did he say why, Bryerton?"

The butler's long nose was high. "I am certain I could not say, Miss Watkin."

She should have known better than to ask. She thought carefully how to phrase the next question as she puffed up the sleeves of her green-sprigged muslin gown where the pelisse had flattened the lace edgings. "Can you say whether Mr. Darby has been here this morning?" she tried.

"He called on your father," Bryerton answered. By the light in his gray eyes, she had the feeling he knew exactly how much that information meant to her.

"And the nature of that conversation?" she asked carefully.

"Is not something to which I was privy. If you would follow me?"

Follow him and have him hear that Jareth had confessed all? She thought not. "No, thank you, Bryerton. I know the way to my father's study."

Bryerton drew himself up and walked away

without another word. No longer caring whether she insulted him, Eloise gathered up her full skirts and hurried down the corridor and up the stairs.

At the door to her father's study, she paused to smooth the curls back from her face. She could feel her heart pounding in her chest and knew it wasn't from climbing the stairs. What would she face inside that door if Jareth had explained their situation to her father? She should have been more forceful in her warning to him last night. But the very fact that he truly did wish to marry her had stunned her.

She wanted to be happy about that. Jareth Darby claimed to be in love, and in love with her. Why didn't that delight her beyond words? Isn't that what she'd hoped for for years? If she were truly honest with herself, wasn't that why she had derived those silly tests to begin with? She'd wanted him to have a change of heart, and miracle of miracles, that was exactly what had happened. But when it came down to asking her father for her hand, she had refused.

It was ridiculous. A part of her was glad Jareth had seen through her fear and come calling anyway. But the far larger part of her stood trembling outside the door of the study, cursing him for putting her in this position. Their past was over. Why should she have to face it with her father?

She almost turned to leave, then remembered that her father had asked for her. She had no choice but to walk through that door. Steeling herself, she hazarded a knock. At her father's call to enter, she stepped boldly through the door on shaking limbs and shut the panel firmly behind her.

"You asked for me, Father?" she asked, bracing herself against the door for strength.

He smiled and indicated the chair before his desk. "Yes, my dear. Please sit down."

The air in the room was warm yet she felt chilled. She did not budge from the door. "Is something wrong?"

"Now why would you think that? Do I only call for you when there is trouble?"

"Well," she admitted, shifting nervously, "the number of times you have called for more frivolous reasons is limited."

"Is that true?" He frowned thoughtfully. "How very remiss of me. I shall attempt to rectify that in the future. For now, please take a seat. I would like you to tell me how you know Jareth Darby."

She had moved toward the chair but his last words caused her to sink onto the hardwood seat with a bump. "Jareth Darby?" she managed. "Why would you ask after him?"

"He was here this morning to see me. He wished my permission to offer for you."

Her heart could not help but leap at the confirmation. "And did you grant it?"

"Reluctantly. The fellow is charming enough, I suppose. However, his confession that he had seduced you while you were still in school was a bit daunting."

Eloise gripped the arms of the chair, knowing her face must be ashen. This was so much worse than she thought. She could see her father's brows drawing into a deeper frown. "Father, I . . ." She swallowed. "I don't know what to say."

"Is it true, then?"

Lie! Her brain shouted. *Tell him a story, lead him*

away from the truth. He could never understand the choices you made. He will despise you if he knows. The fears crowded around her until her shoulders slumped under the weight.

"Eloise?" Her father's voice was gentle. "Will you answer me, please?"

She met his gaze, no warmer now than the day her mother had died. What truly did she risk? She had lost his love long ago.

"Yes, Father," she said. "It is true."

"I see," he replied with the same thoughtful tone. "And why did you not tell me sooner?"

She sucked in a breath. "Miss Martingale forbade it. She thought I had led him on, you see. She thought I was trying to trap him into marriage."

He rose abruptly and went to look out the window, hands clasped behind his back. She could see his fingers curling in a pale sickle against the brown of his wool coat. "And what would you have told me if you had been allowed?" he asked the glass of the window.

She hesitated. What good did it do to bring it all up now? In truth, she wanted only to forget the past. Yet something in his manner told her that he very much wanted to know. She swallowed the lump that persisted in her throat. "I would have told you that I was alone and frightened. That I was afraid you would despise me for what I'd done, just as Miss Martingale seemed to despise me. I would have begged you to understand that I was so in love I could have refused him nothing. That I believed my choice was right. Very likely I would have pleaded with you to find him and return him to me. I'm sure you would have been able to tell that at that moment I would have done anything to be loved."

Her father's shoulders bowed as if she had somehow transferred her burden to him. Indeed, she marveled that she felt lighter. His voice was grave. "I seem to have failed you when you needed me most."

"No," she replied, refusing to blame him. "You could not know. And later, I didn't have the strength to tell you."

"I should have asked." He turned to eye her, his face set in deep lines. "I have felt for some time that there were things left unsaid between us. I thought perhaps it was your mother's death, but I can no more talk of that now than when she died over ten years ago."

"I understand, Father," she said, although in truth, she had never been able to understand why they had drifted apart.

"Do you? Then I have done a far better job than I suspected of raising you." He shook his head. "But I did not raise you, did I, Eloise? I left it entirely too much to the hands of others. Talented others for the most part, but others to be sure. What else have I missed in your life?"

"Nothing of import," she assured him. "You know about my troubles before Cleo befriended me last Season."

He nodded. "I remember Lord Hastings assuring me that the *ton* had begun to think you fast. Perhaps you were still looking for that love you were denied."

She shook her head, more to remove that vision of herself than to argue with him. "I have changed, Father. I am attempting to be a woman who can be respected. I have friends now and suitors who claim to care. I no longer need to chase after love."

She was shocked to see tears pooling in his eyes. "You should never have had to chase it, Eloise. You should have grown up knowing you were loved. I have no one to blame but myself if you did not."

"Father," she started, her voice rough with the emotions she felt building.

He held up a hand. "Hear me out. I am not a demonstrative man, Eloise. Very likely I did not show you the attention you could have expected from your mother. But I love you, with all my heart. Nothing could ever change that. Please forgive me for making you doubt that." He opened his arms.

She stared at him, stunned, but there could be no mistaking his gesture. Rising, she met him halfway and fell into his arms. Her father held her so close she could feel the warmth of his wool coat against her cheek, see it darken from the tears that coursed down her cheeks. One hand patted her back awkwardly, and he murmured words of comfort as if she were a child again.

And, just for a moment, she was a child again. A frightened, lonely child, abandoned by everyone who had claimed to love her. She sobbed against her father's shoulder, crying out the pain of years of fear, regret, confusion, and longing. She cried for the child she had been and the woman she would have become but for Cleo's friendship and her own determination. She cried for the woman she still might become if she could not find the courage to love again.

And in that instant, she realized why that courage was so very hard to find. She had thought she had put her past behind her. She had thought she was focusing on becoming a woman of character. She had forgiven Cleo for the times her friend had doubted her. In her heart, she had already forgiven Jareth. This moment she released any hurt she had been harboring against her father. What she had never faced was the hurt she had caused herself.

She had made her choice those years ago and worked her way through the consequences. But some part of her was angry, angry at Jareth, angry at Cleo, angry at her father, but most of all angry at herself. She should have been smarter, she should have seen more clearly what would happen if she indulged her passionate heart. She saw those arguments now for what they were: the pain of a lonely child. She was no longer that child. She was the woman of character she had dreamed of becoming. She surrendered the last of her pain and resolved to look only toward the future and what more she might become.

She straightened out of her father's arms. His cheeks were as damp as her own. She wiped at her face with her fingers.

"Thank you, Father."

He smiled, laying a hand on her shoulder as if to prevent her from pulling any farther away. "Thank *you*, my dear. I shall endeavor to never again cause you to doubt my love."

She returned his smile and laid her own hand on his in a pledge. "And I hope I never give you cause to doubt mine."

"I am certain that will never happen," he replied, releasing her at last. "And in that regard, would you like me to make Jareth Darby disappear?"

"Have you a magic wand, Father?" she teased as she returned to the chair.

"No, but a number of good friends and connections. Has he hurt you?"

She paused. Feeling for the pain, she was surprised and pleased to find that it had disappeared. "Not recently," she replied. "And I do believe he has changed."

Her father was watching her closely. "Then you would welcome this suit?"

She smiled. "Yes. Though I wonder whether there might be too much between us. He is a rogue. Yet I think if I had not known him before I would still be charmed by him. He sees the ridiculous in every situation. He lives life on his own terms, but not in defiance, in supreme self-confidence, shackled only by his own convictions, however skewed."

"And I believe some young ladies find him attractive."

"*All* ladies find him attractive," she corrected him with a wry grin. "Young and old alike. Yet though I know I must be one of many, he has a way of making me feel as if I am the only one whose opinion he values." She stopped herself. "Do you hear me, Father? Despite my best efforts to hold myself away from him, he has managed to gain a hold on my heart."

Her father cocked his head, birdlike. "Does this disturb you?"

"It should! Look at the wreck he made of my life the last time he appeared. And yet, if he asked

me this moment to marry him, I would answer
yes."

He nodded. "Mr. Darby is a fortunate man. I
am glad he insisted I talk with you."

"Jareth insisted we talk?" She frowned. "Why?"

"He seemed to feel you needed my support.
He was obviously quite right. In that, we both owe
him a debt of thanks."

"I suppose we do," she marveled. Indeed, it
was the most unselfish thing she had ever known
Jareth to do.

"You need not fear him, you know," her father
continued. "Surely you see that the situation is
completely different this time. Then you were in-
experienced, alone, and defenseless. Now you are
a confident young woman, you have friends and
family behind you, and you are quite able to de-
fend yourself. Follow your heart and you have
nothing to fear."

His logic wrung a laugh from her. "But Father,
my heart is exactly the problem!"

He smiled at her. "Because it says Mr. Darby is
to be trusted this time?"

"Precisely!"

"Why is that wrong?"

So many reasons flooded her mind. He had betrayed her, he had dallied with other women, he
had run away to the Continent, he sought her
only for her forgiveness. But as she considered
each, she realized they were all founded on the
fears of the past, fears she no longer needed to
heed. Since his return, Jareth had repeatedly
proven himself a gentleman, someone worthy of
her trust, someone worthy of her love. He had
never attempted to harm her and, indeed, had

often made her laugh. He had consistently put her needs before his own—going through with her tests, breaking off kisses to suit her, even urging her father to help her.

Yet she felt as if Jareth were hiding something from her. There was the way he had reacted when she suggested that money motivated him to seek her forgiveness, and the way he refused to meet her gaze when explaining why he had never returned for her. She could think of no good reason to explain those actions, but neither could she think of a nefarious one. Surely these feelings of hers were only more ghosts from the past. She should ignore them until she had reason to do otherwise.

She leaned over and kissed her father on the cheek. "Thank you, Father. You are right, of course. There is nothing wrong with trusting Mr. Darby. If he decides to call and make an offer, I shall listen carefully and trust my heart to answer."

Nineteen

Eloise had just finished luncheon with her father when Bryerton announced that she had a visitor. Her father smiled at her, but she felt her heart leap into her throat. She rose from her seat as the butler continued.

"Miss Sinclair is here, Miss Eloise."

She froze. "Miss Sinclair?"

"Miss Portia Sinclair," he intoned. "She is in the sitting room, alone."

She had all but forgotten Portia Sinclair and her attempt to entrap Jareth in marriage. She had little interest in seeing the girl, but she couldn't find it in her to send her off. Excusing herself, she went downstairs.

Her first thought on entering the sitting room was that Portia looked horrid. The girl's face, framed by a straw bonnet, was blotchy, her eyes swollen and red-rimmed. She kept clenching and unclenching her hands in the lap of her pink cotton gown and when Eloise moved forward to greet her, she shot to her feet as if guilty of being caught in some indiscretion.

"How can I help you, Miss Sinclair?" Eloise asked, taking a seat on the closest chair and nodding to the girl to sit down again opposite her.

Instead, Portia threw herself down beside Eloise and turned soulful eyes her way.

"Oh, Miss Watkin, I had to speak with you. Even though we are not well known to each other, I have sensed a refinement of spirit in you that tells me you will understand my plight."

"Your plight?" Eloise probed, wondering whether the girl meant to confess her plot against Jareth.

She nodded, digging in her pink satin reticule to produce a silken handkerchief with which to dab at her eyes. "Yes. You see, I have fallen in love, but the gentleman does not return the sentiment."

Small wonder, if she chose to show her admiration by attempting to trap the fellow into marriage. "I imagine there are many young ladies who would understand falling in love in vain. It seems the nature of the Season."

"Oh, indeed. But I must admit to my own naiveté. You see, I believed he cared, and I allowed him to take certain liberties with my person."

Eloise refused to encourage her by looking shocked. "Such things happen."

"So I have heard. But I fear my father will not be so understanding. I fear . . . that is, I believe . . . oh, Miss Watkin, I am in the family way."

Eloise felt cold all over. "Then the gentleman must be persuaded to do his duty."

Tears fell to dot her dress a deeper rose. "Oh no, he cannot. And Mr. Darby has made it clear that he despises me and wants nothing more to do with me."

The girl's shoulders shook as she bent over the handkerchief, the corner of which was neatly

monogrammed with the letters JD. Eloise stared
at them. Her intellect readily seized on the evidence. Here at last was the proof that Jareth had
not changed after all, proof that he was despicable, that he was heartless. Yet her own heart protested. He had told her he was innocent of this.
If she loved him, she had to believe him.

But asking Portia whether she was certain her
betrayer was Jareth seemed pointless at best and
cruel at worst. Unfortunately, it was just as hard
to believe the girl was set on entrapment as it was
to believe Jareth was innocent. Her sorrow
seemed very real to Eloise. In fact, Eloise could
not seem to help feeling it inside.

"It is devastating when men are so cruel," she
told Portia. "They either do not know or do not
care the damage they leave behind."

Portia nodded, sniffing. "I was certain you
would understand."

"Better than you can know. And from my experience, I can tell you that you must draw on
your own strength, and that of God above, to see
you through this."

"And my dear friends like you, Miss Watkin,"
she amended, raising a tear-streaked face.

"And your family," Eloise insisted. "You must
not fear to talk to them."

"I could never tell my father," Portia said with
a shudder that shook her slender shoulders anew.
"And my stepmother has been insistent that I resolve the issue. I am not sure of her support. May
I count on yours?"

"I will do all I can to help you, Miss Sinclair."

Her gaze was worshipful. "Then you will speak
to Jareth for me?"

Eloise blinked. "Speak to Jareth?"

She nodded. "Yes, please. Tell him about my concerns. Tell him how much I need him."

Eloise felt as if a rock had lodged in the pit of her stomach. The yearning she saw in Portia's soft gray gaze, the throb of desperation in her voice—she had lived them. How could she possibly refuse? Yet, if she believed Jareth, she had to refuse. "I could not possibly plead your case."

Portia took her hands in her damp ones. "But you must, Miss Watkin. I can think of no more eloquent champion. I know Mr. Darby highly esteems you. Surely he will listen to you."

"This truly should be a matter between the two of you," Eloise insisted. "You must talk with him yourself."

Her eyes filled with tears again. "I cannot bear it! He is so firm in his resolve and his moods frighten me."

"Indeed," Eloise said, extracting her hands from the girl's clammy grip. "Then I wonder that you wish to be reunited with him."

"I would not so wish, but for the child," she replied, dropping her gaze. "Surely my baby deserves better than to be born a bastard."

Eloise flinched, but stood her ground. "Better to bear a bastard, Miss Sinclair, than marry one. Besides, if you only had the one moment of passion with Mr. Darby a few days ago, it is much too soon to be certain that you have conceived a child, and not all that likely either, as I understand it."

Portia crumpled the handkerchief, keeping her gaze downcast. "The incident at Lady Wenworth's was but the last of a string of encounters. I fear

I fell in love with Mr. Darby at first sight, several days before the night he startled you at Almack's. He was so dashing, so charming, so persistent that I was swept away."

"Yes, Mr. Darby has that effect on people," Eloise acknowledged, mind whirling. Could it be true? Could Jareth have been carrying on with Portia Sinclair from the start? Her mind willingly conjured up any number of exchanged smiles and furtive touches. Yet she also remembered how cool he had been to Portia recently, compared to the warmth and good humor he had shown her. Had it all been a sham over the last month?

"Then you will speak to him?"

She must, if only to hear his side of the story. Eloise nodded. "I shall discuss the matter with Mr. Darby this very day. But I make no promise about the outcome, Miss Sinclair. I should not like to advise him against his best interests."

"But surely it is in his best interests to take responsibility for his actions," she protested. "Surely you would want him to provide for this child."

"Certainly," Eloise replied readily, though she was not ready to admit there was a child as yet. "At the very least I can contrive to have him discuss the matter with you as he should."

"Oh, Miss Watkin," she breathed, "you are an angel."

"Nonsense," Eloise replied, remembering all too well how Jareth was wont to use the name. "Now, you should go home and get some rest. Return tomorrow at this time and we shall see what can be done."

Portia rose and Eloise rose with her. The girl

threw her arms about Eloise and hugged her close. Eloise stiffened. Portia hastily let go.

"Forgive me for being so familiar. I am over-wrought. Thank you, thank you, dear Miss Watkin! I shall see you on the morrow and I shall pray for a happy end."

Eloise nodded, moving to open the door for her. A waiting footman stepped forward to see her out. Eloise turned from them and went to sink back upon the chair she had vacated.

Incongruously, her heart demanded that she believe in Jareth, in the love he had confessed, and the love she felt for him. But how could she reconcile that love with what she now knew to be true?

For when Portia had hugged her, their bellies had brushed. Under the high-waisted gown, Portia was blossoming. Portia Sinclair was indeed with child.

Could Jareth be the father?

She would have liked nothing better than to hide away and think. Between the confession with her father and Portia's revelation, she hardly knew her own mind. Unfortunately, she had no sooner retired to her room than she found she had another caller.

Martha brought her the news. "Lord Peter Nathaniel to see you, Miss," she said after rapping at the door and being bid to enter. Eloise would have liked to tell him to call another time, but as Bryerton had already apparently told him she was home, she was honor-bound to greet him. She rose wearily to follow Martha back down the stairs, but something in her maid's manner stopped her.

The woman's mouth was even tighter than usual and she stood like a statue in her black uniform.

"Is something troubling you, Martha?" Eloise asked.

Her maid kept her gaze on the floor. "I'm sure I couldn't say, Miss Watkin."

All at once Eloise had had enough. If she and her father could develop a satisfactory relationship, why should she hesitate to tell her servant what she desired? She planted herself directly in front of the woman. "But I am asking you to say what's troubling you. You oversee some of the most intimate moments of my life, Martha. If you have knowledge that concerns me, I wish you to tell me."

Martha stiffened even more, if that were possible. "Mr. Bryerton has other ideas on the running of the household," she muttered with her usual glower. "I would not like to cross him."

"You leave Mr. Bryerton to me. While I respect his position as head of the household staff, I have needs that must be met. Now, please, Martha, tell me what's wrong."

Martha hesitated a moment more. Then her carriage relaxed and she raised her head to meet Eloise's gaze. Eloise was surprised to see a smile beaming from Martha's square-jawed face.

"While you were with Miss Sinclair, Lord Nathaniel called on your father," she confided, excitement evident in the way her large hands trembled as they came together before her. "I hope we shall soon have cause to wish you happy, Miss Watkin."

Eloise didn't have the heart to disappoint her. Martha pleasant was far too precious to waste.

Still, she could not set up false expectations. "I hope so too, Martha. Though perhaps my happiness lies with a different gentleman."

Martha's dark eyes were knowing. "Mr. Darby beat his lordship out, did he? Good for you, Miss Watkin, for getting that gentleman to offer a ring at last."

Eloise shared her smile. "Thank you, Martha, though in truth he hasn't offered that ring just yet. I expect him later today. Now I'd better go break the news to Lord Nathaniel."

She wasn't entirely sure how she would go about it, but that conversation also proved easier than she had thought. The viscount was pacing the garden withdrawing room when she entered, his brown coat dark against the pale walls. As soon as he saw her, he rushed to her side. Face flushed, he started to drop to one knee. Eloise braced her hands on his broad shoulders to stop him.

"Please, my lord, won't you sit beside me on the sofa? I think we would be more comfortable there."

He heaved himself back to his feet. "Certainly, certainly, if that is what you wish."

Eloise spread the skirts of her green-sprigged muslin gown to sit. Lord Nathaniel perched on the opposite side of the sofa. He eyed her warily as if he saw the change in her. She wondered if her new-found confidence was so obvious.

"You intend to refuse," he guessed, clasping his hands together as if to keep them from trembling.

Eloise was ready to agree straight out, but for some reason, Jareth's advice about the fragility of gentlemen's feelings came to mind. Perhaps she should try to keep his pride intact.

She lowered her gaze. "You honor me by speaking to my father, Lord Nathaniel," she murmured. "Had I realized sooner that that was your intention, my decision might have been different."

"Darby," he said. "Drat his eyes. I was afraid he had stolen a march on me. But with the scandal over Miss Portia Sinclair, I thought perhaps you might see him differently."

"Oh, I do, I assure you. He will never be the man you are, my lord, but I find myself content with that."

He heaved a sigh. "I hope that we can remain friends at least."

Eloise assured him that she felt the same way and rose to see him out. As the door closed behind him, she shook her head in wonder. Gentlemen certainly took disappointment well when one cradled their pride.

She paused on her way up the stairs. Pride. That infamous Darby pride. Even Lady DeGuis had remarked upon it. Jareth made light of things so easily that she had not thought him infected, but she saw now that she had been wrong. It had been pride that drove him away from her and pride that kept him from returning afterward. Could pride be associated with his reaction to the mention of money?

The more she thought about it, the more convinced she became. He surely had no money. Had she in fact seen him spend a penny since arriving in London? He had sent her flowers, but he might have gotten those from a Darby hothouse. Certainly he had a limited wardrobe and she had yet to see him in a carriage or on horseback. She hadn't even seen him enter the Fenton, when she thought on it. For all she knew, he slept in Hyde Park!

But surely his future was not so bleak. Pride may have kept him from taking charity from his brother, but she did not think his stories of Cheddar Cliffs were untrue. His eyes glowed when he talked of the estate. But he could not claim it until she granted forgiveness. He had stayed in London, in near poverty, on her whim.

She shook her head again, continuing upstairs. They both had much to learn. She only hoped they might learn it together. In refusing Lord Nathaniel, she had cleared the way for Jareth to make his declaration. His pride had kept him from committing himself to her last time.

Would he actually take that step now?

Twenty

Jareth was none too sure of his chances when he arrived at the Watkin townhouse that afternoon in his best blue velvet suit. Although Eloise's father had not been particularly discouraging, his own experiences with Eloise of late had been too volatile to assure him of success. In fact, the only person who seemed certain of the outcome was Eleanor.

"If she is the lady for you, you will succeed," his sister-in-law predicted. "Look at Adam and Helena. Look at Alex and Patricia. For that matter, look at Justinian and me."

Jareth had grinned. "Now *that* was an interesting courtship. It took my brother only, what, fifteen years to pop the question?"

"Precisely. If we could find our way together, so can you and Miss Watkin. Let me know when we may wish you happy. I would be delighted to throw you an engagement ball."

Jareth knew he was lucky. Given the situation with Portia Sinclair, his sister-in-law could just as likely be happier throwing things at him as for him.

Mrs. Sinclair had been adamant that he offer for Portia. He had, of course, refused. The despair in Portia Sinclair's eyes had cut him to the quick. Yet he knew he had not caused her pain. Her problems were not his responsibility.

But his refusal had not been accepted. He remembered how Mrs. Sinclair had puffed out her chest when he and Justinian had met with her.

"What other alternatives can there be, my lord?" she had demanded. "Do you think you can possibly pay me enough money to look the other way?"

Justinian had lifted a brow even as Jareth folded his arms over his chest.

"Who mentioned money, Mrs. Sinclair?" he challenged.

She shook her head. "I am not so naïve as that, Mr. Darby. When a girl has been ruined, there is a price to be paid, either in marriage or in restitution. If you will not have the one, it stands to reason you must have the other."

Jareth quirked a smile. "Very well, Mrs. Sinclair. You can have my entire fortune."

He was not surprised by the greed that lit her narrow little eyes. He stepped up to her and took her hand. Holding it palm up, he reached into the pocket of his waistcoat and fished around. With a flourish, he handed her a shilling, pressing it deeply into the flabby folds in his grip. He closed her fingers over it.

"Guard it well, my dear," he cautioned. "You never know when someone's going to cheat you of it."

"Jareth," Justinian growled in warning.

He stepped back from Mrs. Sinclair, but not before he saw her face flush with anger. She threw the coin on the floor and stormed out.

She had since sent a note stating that she expected to hear their resolution by the end of the week. He would not waiver. Justinian and Eleanor were united in their support of him. He refused to let them down. Neither would he let Eloise down. He could not lose her now.

The thought was a burning coal in his gut. He could not lose Eloise! She made him feel things no other woman made him feel. She made him look at the world with more compassion than he had thought possible. Being with her made him a better person. Cheddar Cliffs, money in his pocket, his family's good will, none of it mattered if he lost Eloise. Indeed, he could not imagine life without her. He was well and truly reformed.

He patted the pocket of his embroidered waistcoat as he waited in the Watkin withdrawing room. His last possession of any worth had been the signet ring his father had given him. But losing it was a small price to pay for the engagement ring that nestled in his pocket. The center diamond wasn't too large or ostentatious, and the emeralds surrounding it matched the green of Eloise's eyes. He hoped she would be pleased with it.

That she was not pleased with something was evident by the way she entered. Her walk was hesitant, her gaze on the Oriental carpet at her feet. It was all he could do to keep from running to her and taking her in his arms. When he realized the butler was nowhere in sight, he knew he was in trouble.

"Do you have designs on my virtue, madam?" he tried joking.

She took the seat farthest from him. "I thought you wished to discuss *your* designs, Mr. Darby."

He moved to sit closer to her. She leaned back. Refusing to be defeated, he reached out and took her hands. They were icy in his grip.

"I have made my designs transparent," he assured her. "I love you and I wish to spend the rest of my life with you." He fished in his pocket, pulled out the ring, and handed it to her.

Eloise stared at it. Her lower lip trembled, but she gave no other sign that his confession had moved her. "What of Portia Sinclair?" she asked simply.

He frowned, releasing her hand. "She is perfectly welcome to do as she pleases. I have no use for her."

She flinched and dropped her gaze. One hand stroked the ring as if she longed to put it on her finger. He knew he would have felt better had she done so.

"Yes, Miss Sinclair seems aware of your feelings," she said in that quiet voice. "Did you know she was with child?"

Jareth started. "No. But that actually explains a great deal."

"Does it?" She gave a bitter laugh. "Then perhaps you would be so good as to explain it to me, for I find myself quite at a loss."

He could see the knowledge of Portia's state had upset her and could easily guess why. She was afraid he was the father. As he had feared, he could still lose her. But protesting his innocence would likely make him only look more the villain. He would have to trust her to think through the facts in the situation. "I would be delighted to explain the matter. You are certain Miss Sinclair is with child?"

She nodded, face drawn. "Oh, yes. I have seen the evidence, so to speak."

"And how long have I been in London?"

She frowned. "Perhaps a month."

"You know that for a fact?"

She cocked her head as if in thought. "No, but I suspect I could confirm it with Lady Wenworth."

"You could indeed. Let us say six weeks just to be conservative. How long does it take after conception for the woman's body to begin to change?"

She lifted her nose. "I certainly have no idea."

"I do. There were times in my life when it was critical to know such things."

She eyed him. "I would imagine."

He could not help giving her a grin. "Then we are agreed that I am an expert on the matter?"

Her mouth quirked, but she did not break into a smile. "We are agreed that I could *find* an expert to confirm your statements."

"Good enough," Jareth replied. "The time until the pregnancy is obvious is between three and five months, depending on the size of the lady and the babe, and whether this is her first or later child. How is it possible, even if I were to have pounced upon Miss Sinclair the moment I left the Channel packet, that she should be obvious in her state in a mere six weeks?"

She stared at him a moment, then, to his surprise, she threw her arms about him.

"Oh, Jareth, I knew you were innocent! My heart wanted to shout it to the stars but my damnable brain kept arguing."

"Perfectly understandable, my love," he said, enjoying the feeling of her willing against him and marveling at it. "I have been a bit of a cad in the past."

"Not such a scoundrel as this," she replied, pulling back with a serious face. "Someone has gotten her with child. Perhaps she does not understand the dates either, but the fact remains that she is to give birth."

"Oh, I have little doubt she understands the calendar as well as I do," Jareth said with a rueful shake of his head. "I also have little doubt that I was carefully chosen to star in her little drama."

Eloise frowned. "What do you mean?"

"My damnable reputation precedes me," Jareth explained. "Who but you will doubt Portia's tale that I fathered her babe?"

"But the dates, her state?" she protested.

"Verifiable by you, but unknown to most. Did she flaunt her belly?"

"By no means. I realized the truth only by accident."

He spread his hands. "And there you have it. As neat a trap as one could want. After seeing her hanging on me at Almack's and finding us alone together at the literary reception, who will doubt that I wasn't dallying with her? Even my silence is against me. Her stepmother demands that I offer."

Eloise sobered. "Indeed, Miss Sinclair came to see me today to beg me to ensure that you did so."

He could see the hurt in her eyes and silently berated Portia and her stepmother for their part in putting it there. He took her gently by the shoulders. "I am so sorry she made you part of this, my love. I should have dealt with her directly."

Eloise did not pull away. "Yes, you should. She will be here at three tomorrow. You must confront her then."

He released her with a resigned nod. "If it pleases you."

"My pleasure is not the issue. She is intent on having you."

"She cannot have me." He brought her hand to his lips. "My heart is yours."

She shivered at his kiss, but he did not think it was fear of him that shook her. "But her need is greater," she insisted. "Much as I despise her tactics, I understand her despair. Someone has used and abandoned her. I have lived that pain. I cannot watch another go through it."

Jareth cradled her hand in his. "What do you ask of me?"

"To put someone's needs before your own."

Her gaze was intent but Jareth felt cold. "Is that your final test? You would have me marry Portia Sinclair?"

She squeezed his hand. "What, Mr. Darby, after you had spoken to my father?" She blinked and grinned. "My goodness, I seem to have borrowed your gift of making light of things."

"At least one of us can do so," he replied, but he felt a smile forming at her pleasure. "I take it you have some other reparation in mind then."

Her smile faded. "No, but something must be done, Jareth. The man responsible must be brought to take responsibility."

"I find it difficult to care. In my book, Miss

Sinclair seeks only to further her own interests and damn the consequences to anyone else."

She raised a black brow. "And does that not sound like someone you once knew?"

He stared at her. She touched his cheek.

"You know the truth, Jareth. And I know you have the strength to do the right thing. I would not love you so much if it were not true."

Her words halted all other thoughts. "You love me? Do I understand you correctly?"

She nodded with a smile, looking suddenly shy. She picked up the ring as if to prove it and slipped it on her finger. "I do. I don't think I ever stopped, through all of it." She seemed about to go on, but he stopped her with a kiss. In it, he felt all his hopes and dreams answered. The fire and the passion he remembered from their past were there, but built now on a foundation of love. When she at last pulled away, they were both breathless.

She laid her hand against his cheek, her touch as warm as their embrace. "We have found our love, Jareth. But you cannot ask me to sit by and watch Portia Sinclair go through such pain. Will you at least come by tomorrow and meet with her? She deserves that much."

He inclined his head. "I will speak with her. But I want no misconceptions that I will give in to this blackmail she appears to be planning. As long as you believe me, I care nothing for what others think. Let Miss Sinclair do her worst."

"She may at that. She is desperate, Jareth. I know the feeling."

"Watch that your feelings do not blind you to her schemes. I will not be trapped."

She stared at him, arrested. He could almost see the thoughts spinning behind her eyes. He had hoped she'd use her intellect, and she certainly seemed to be justifying that hope. A smile spread on her lovely face. "My dear Mr. Darby, you are so clever. I do not know why I did not appreciate it sooner."

He cocked his head. "What do you mean? Did I say something to give you an idea of how to handle Miss Sinclair?"

"You did indeed. You are quite right that you should not be trapped. But I begin to believe I know who should. Be here tomorrow and we will endeavor to catch the culprit in her own net."

Twenty-one

By the following afternoon, Eloise could only hope she had done the right thing. As soon as she had gotten Jareth out of the house, she had hurried to Cleo's to enlist her friend's help. It had taken some doing to convince Cleo of Jareth's innocence, but the fact that Eloise wore his ring proudly on her finger went a long way toward making Cleo see that perhaps he might be redeemable.

Once Cleo was convinced, they set about enlisting Leslie's support. His father had been the head of an elite group of spies and every one of them was inclined to do his son a favor. A few words in the right ears netted a great deal of information. A fast horse out the Dover Road made Eloise hope that more information might arrive before their meeting.

She hesitated to tell her father of her activities, but she realized that if she were to keep developing the relationship they had rekindled that morning, she had to ignore her fears of his censure. She forced herself to knock at his study door.

"I wanted you to know what happened this afternoon with Lord Nathaniel and Jareth Darby," she explained after he had greeted her.

"I take it by your hesitation that you refused them both," her father guessed.

"I refused Lord Nathaniel." She held out her hand to show him the ring Jareth had given her. "This is Mr. Darby's ring. Before we can marry, however, we must solve a problem." She went on to explain the situation with Portia Sinclair and her plans to resolve it.

He listened solemnly, asked a few questions, then nodded. "A very wise plan of action. I am proud of you, Eloise. But then, I am always proud of you." He offered her a hug, which she gladly accepted.

"By the by," he added as they separated, "I understand you and Bryerton are having a tiff."

She grimaced. "I had been so busy I had forgotten to speak with him. I fear I insulted him, and I certainly cannot change your expectations for the staff but I cannot abide how he insists upon escorting me about my own house."

Her father nodded thoughtfully. "I will speak to him. I did not realize how easily I slip into formality. Very likely because I lived here alone for a time before you returned from school, he sees you more as a guest than family. You need not feel you must have his permission to see me."

"Thank you, Father," she replied with a smile of relief. "I hope you can convince him to continue in his other duties. He is rather good at keeping unwanted guests away."

"I am certain he will agree. He is too much the professional to do otherwise."

Although Bryerton was the least of her problems, she had gone to bed that night feeling far lighter than she had in years. She had kissed the ring on her finger for luck before falling asleep.

Now, as the meeting time approached, Eloise found her hands sweating and her mouth dry. She must have rearranged the skirts of her lilac lustring dress three times before the clock struck the hour.

Cleo arrived first, as planned. She burst into the withdrawing room in a flurry of saffron skirts.

"No news from Dover," she confirmed after allowing Bryerton to do his duty and announce her. "But Les has instructions to send on anyone who arrives before I return home."

Jareth was the next to arrive, handsome as always in his navy coat. He looked a little surprised to see Cleo, but he bowed to her before going to kiss Eloise's palm. Cleo bristled, but Jareth winked at Eloise as if to let her know he did not care who knew where his feelings lay.

She wondered whether she could keep the two of them away from each other's throat while they waited for Portia. Before she knew it, however, Jareth was telling a story that set her to giggling. He soon had Cleo in stitches. When Portia Sinclair arrived, they were a merry group indeed. She looked startled that the three of them should be so happy at such a time, but her stepmother behind her looked positively ominous.

She stopped her stepdaughter from moving forward as Bryerton attempted to usher them into the room.

"Mrs. and Miss Sinclair," he announced, then hurriedly bowed himself out.

"I do not understand," Mrs. Sinclair said, raising her head above the white ruffled collar of her navy gown. "I thought this conversation was about Mr. Darby and my stepdaughter. Why do you have other company, Miss Watkin?"

Cleo rose, as did Jareth. Smiling pleasantly, she went to take Portia's hands to pull her into the room, all the while chatting with her stepmother. "Please let me stay, Mrs. Sinclair. I am here to see that justice is done."

Mrs. Sinclair frowned as if not trusting the situation.

"Justice?" Portia asked, sinking in a cloud of pink muslin onto the chair to which Cleo led her.

"Yes, justice," Eloise confirmed. She gestured to Mrs. Sinclair to take a seat near Portia. "I took the liberty of letting Lady Wenworth know of Miss Sinclair's predicament and she is as adamant as I am that you receive the right help."

"Why . . . how kind," Portia said, gaze darting between the two of them.

"How kind indeed," Mrs. Sinclair muttered, though she looked no less skeptical.

"We are," Cleo warbled, "kind to a fault. And speaking of faults, Miss Sinclair, I understand you believe we should lay the fault squarely at Mr. Darby's door."

"I'm sure I never said," Portia started, but her stepmother interrupted.

"Mr. Darby has refused to bear responsibility for his dalliance with my stepdaughter," she said, her short nose high. "I had to restrain Mr. Sinclair from calling him out."

"I am certain no one wants bloodshed," Eloise said, though she rather thought Jareth could hold his own if needed.

"Only my blood," Jareth put in, "as the sacrificial lamb."

Mrs. Sinclair sputtered, but he continued before Eloise could caution him. "You know as well as I do that I have no responsibility to bear, Mrs. Sinclair. Your stepdaughter and I have only a passing acquaintance." His gaze at the girl was steely, and Eloise could see her swallow.

"Come now, Mr. Darby," Eloise chided, forcing herself to focus on their goals. "I am certain you know her better than that. And as a friend, you will surely wish to see justice done as much as Lady Hastings and I do."

He frowned at her while Mrs. Sinclair measured him with narrowed eyes. "Justice, certainly," he allowed. "Although I would wager we have a different opinion on what constitutes justice."

"Perhaps not so different as you might think," Eloise murmured.

"In any event," Cleo put in before Mrs. Sinclair could start further protests, "I believe we are agreed as to our purpose."

"Assuredly," Eloise said. "We are intent on making the father of the child responsible."

Portia flinched but her stepmother nodded, leaning back in the chair with obvious satisfaction. "That is exactly what I desire as well."

Eloise smiled. "Good. Then you will not mind telling us when last your stepdaughter saw Major Churchill."

She blinked, paling. "Major Churchill? I am certain I do not remember. What has he to do with anything?"

Eloise watched the girl. "He is the father, is he not, Portia?"

Mrs. Sinclair surged to her feet. "How dare you! Do you call my dear girl a liar?"

"No," Eloise said quietly. "But I'm not entirely certain about you."

The woman sputtered, but Eloise rose and knelt beside the girl. "Tell the truth, Portia. We will see that you are cared for, I promise."

While Mrs. Sinclair called down imprecations, Portia's gaze darted from face to face as if afraid to hope for a receptive audience. For a moment Eloise thought she might brazen it out. Then she hung her head.

"Yes," she whispered. "Major Churchill is the father."

Jareth grinned.

"You forced her to say that!" Mrs. Sinclair declared, moving to Portia's other side. "Portia, I demand you tell them the truth."

Portia's lower lip trembled, but she refused to meet her stepmother's outraged gaze. "I did tell the truth."

Eloise took Portia's hands in hers, ignoring the angered woman beside them. "I know you did, Portia. That was the hardest part. The next is easier. Has Major Churchill refused to accept responsibility?"

"Stop this at once!" Mrs. Sinclair demanded. She pushed against Eloise, knocking her off balance. She started to fall, only to feel Jareth's arms around her.

"Touch her again," he said to Mrs. Sinclair, "and I will not be responsible for my actions."

Eloise could not see his face, but it must have been magnificent, for Mrs. Sinclair blanched and stumbled back to her seat. Gazing at Eloise, Portia swallowed.

"Major Churchill said he wished to marry me," she said, voice gaining confidence with each word, "but his detachment was recalled to duty. I sent him a note when I realized I was with child, but he never responded. I could not let my child be born a bastard."

"Of course not," Eloise soothed.

"Particularly when I provided you such an easy solution," Jareth murmured behind her.

Eloise squeezed his hand on her shoulder in warning, but Portia sighed.

"I am sorry, Mr. Darby. I did try to set the blame on you. My stepmother insisted on it."

Jareth rose from behind Eloise. "A Darby is worth a great deal more than a half-pay officer, isn't that true, Mrs. Sinclair?"

The woman glowered at him, but Portia shook her head.

"Do not be angry with her, Mr. Darby. She was certain my father would be furious if my state became known."

Eloise was sure Jareth could have argued the point, but he wisely restrained himself.

"You were my only hope," Portia told him, gray eyes solemn. "Thank you for being willing to help."

He nodded. "Always willing to help a lady in distress, Miss Sinclair. Provided, of course, she does not attempt to inflict that distress on others."

She puckered, but nodded as well. "But what can we do?"

"A great deal," Eloise said, rising. "Miss Sinclair, I am going to reunite you with Major Churchill."

"Will you allow me to say nothing in this matter?" Mrs. Sinclair demanded.

"You, madam," Jareth declared, "have forfeited any right to say a word, as far as I'm concerned."

She glowered at him, but apparently realizing that she had lost any leverage in the situation, she lapsed into silence.

"How can you reunite me with Major Churchill?" Portia said to Eloise. "He may no longer want me. He may refuse to do his duty."

"Then we will find somewhere for you to have the baby in quiet," Cleo put in. "My husband is very powerful, Miss Sinclair. You need have no fears. You can live a perfectly normal life in a small town, you and the baby."

"Alone?" Her lower lip trembled.

"Only if necessary," Eloise assured her. "We three will stand by you. Won't we?"

Cleo nodded. Eloise looked at Jareth. She wondered whether the Darby pride would bend in this instance. Surely that would bode well for their future together. Her heart swelled when she saw him nod as well.

"No woman should have to bear a child alone, Miss Sinclair," he said. "You may count on my support, if not my name."

The tears fell. "You are all too kind," she murmured. Cleo rose to take her in her arms.

"There, there, now, Miss Sinclair. It will all come right, you'll see."

Jareth touched Eloise's hand, forcing her to meet his gaze. "Do you know?" he said as she basked in the appreciation in his eyes. "I begin to believe it just might at that."

There was a rap at the door and at Eloise's command, Bryerton entered. "A gentleman here to see you, Miss Watkin. A Major Churchill. He appears to be quite upset. I dared not let him beyond the entry."

Portia hastily stiffened away from Cleo, wiping her cheeks with her sleeve. "Oh no! He's here? He mustn't see me like this!"

"Give us a moment, Bryerton," Eloise instructed, recognizing the girl's need. "Then I think you can safely bring him to us."

As her butler left, Mrs. Sinclair rose. "I refuse to be a party to these proceedings. You are leading my stepdaughter astray. Portia, if you agree to go along with this charade, I wash my hands of you."

Eloise went to Portia, helping her rise. With Cleo on one side and her on the other, Eloise hoped the girl would find the strength to stand up to the woman. Portia bit her lip, but she squared her shoulders.

"I'm sorry, madam, but I must do what is right for me and my child."

Mrs. Sinclair stalked from the room. Eloise gave Portia a squeeze.

"Standing up for yourself gets easier every time you do it, doesn't it?" she said with a smile.

Portia's smile was watery. "Yes, it does, Miss Watkin. But I still do not know whether I can face Major Churchill."

"You must face him," Eloise told her, "whatever his decision. Believe me in this. If you do not, he will haunt you the rest of your life."

Portia nodded, sniffing back tears. A moment later and Bryerton ushered in the major. As Eloise remembered from seeing him at Almack's, he was tall, handsome, and powerfully built. She suspected she would once have been tempted just as Portia must have been. He took in Eloise, Cleo, and Jareth with a frown of confusion. Then his gaze lit on Portia. He rushed forward to take her hands.

"Miss Sinclair, how glad I am to see you here! I was told you were in danger. I came as quickly as I could. What's happened?"

"Oh, Rufus!" Portia fell into his arms, sobbing. The tender way he held her told Eloise everything she needed to know. She motioned to Cleo and Jareth and the three of them tiptoed from the room.

Twenty-two

In the corridor, Jareth shook his head. "So, Major Churchill wasn't a scoundrel either."

"It appears not," Eloise agreed with a smile. "We shall know for sure when they bid us return."

"If I recognized that look in his eye," Jareth said, "we will not be invited back anytime soon."

Cleo sighed with obvious pleasure. "A job well done, my friends."

"Friends?" Jareth raised a brow. "Do you count me as a friend, Lady Hastings?"

"I believe I do, Mr. Darby," she replied. "Until you give me reason to do otherwise."

"Heaven forbid," he said with a laugh. "I have already had a taste of your barbed contempt."

Cleo cringed at the pun. Eloise laughed.

"And you, Miss Watkin?" he challenged. "Do you see me as a friend as well?"

Eloise batted her eyelashes at him. "Oh, no, Mr. Darby. I am certain you are ever so much more than a friend."

"Quite right," he replied. Then he seized her in his arms and set about proving it to her.

"Mr. Darby!" Cleo cried in mock censure. "I may not have a pitchfork, but there is a vase handy if you persist in this demonstration."

He raised his lips from Eloise's but kept her safely in his arms. "You will need a cannon this time, madam. Miss Watkin may have accepted my ring, but she has yet to tell me that she will truly marry me. I vow I will not release her until she has agreed to be my wife."

"Oh, but you make the choice difficult, sir," Eloise teased with a wink to Cleo. "Stay in your arms forever or become your wife? Can I endure such consequences? What if I choose both?"

"Done," Jareth proclaimed, and he went back to kissing her as Cleo clapped in delight. She then behaved just as a good friend ought and found something to busy herself with at the far end of the corridor.

As for Eloise, she found there was nowhere she would rather be than in Jareth's arms. He was obviously not as reformed as he liked to pretend, for his kisses were decidedly not what a gentleman should be giving a lady, even his affianced bride. She decided, however, that she didn't mind in the slightest. Perhaps she had not changed as much as she had thought either. In this area of her life, she rather hoped she never would.

When he at last released her, she could only smile at him in what she was certain must be a most besotted fashion. He looked just as pleased with the matter. "Then you forgive me?" he asked as if to make sure. "You do not require a third test?"

"No," she replied. "I forgive you, and I forgive myself. That last part was far more difficult, I assure you."

He cocked his head. "And just what did you need forgiveness for?"

"For doubting you. For doubting my father and friends. For doubting myself. You have taught me a great deal, my love."

He chuckled. "Not nearly as much as you've taught me, I'd wager."

"What?" she challenged. "A mere slip of a girl teach a Darby anything?"

His arms tightened so that he might nuzzle her neck. "You taught me about true love," he murmured in her ear before planting a kiss there. "That there is far more to this," he illustrated with another kiss, "than simply the joining of two bodies. That I must not let my pride get in the way of that love."

She snuggled against him, well pleased with herself at the thought.

"And you will marry me?" he murmured as if still a little unsure of her.

"As soon as you can produce a license," she promised.

"Will tomorrow be soon enough?"

"Tomorrow?" She gaped at him, then giggled. "Such haste, Mr. Darby. They will suspect we have a reason."

He pulled her back into his arms. "Oh, I have the very best reason of all. Anyone can see I am utterly devoted to you. And if I haven't proven as much to your satisfaction, allow me to spend the rest of my life doing so."

And he did. And so did she.

Dear Reader,

I hope you enjoyed the story of Eloise and Jareth. Love truly is too precious to waste, particularly when you remember to both give and receive.

You may have noticed old friends from my other stories. The courtship of Lord and Lady Hastings is the plot of *The Irredeemable Miss Renfield*, which first introduced Eloise and her scandalous past. Jareth's own past was first introduced in the novella, "A Place by the Fire," in *Mistletoe Kittens*. That story told of how Justinian and Eleanor remembered their love for each other, thanks to the help of a small, black kitten. And my dearest Margaret, Lady DeGuis, first began helping Comfort House in *The Marquis' Kiss*, the book in which she fell in love with a most unlikely gentleman.

If you enjoyed this and my other books, I hope you'll look for my next book, a full-length Regency-set romance entitled *My Heart's Desire*, available from Zebra in June 2003.

I love to hear from readers. Please visit my web site at www.reginascott.com or e-mail me at regina@reginascott.com. If you send me a letter via Zebra, please enclose a self-addressed, stamped envelope if you would like a reply.

Happy reading!
Regina Scott

Celebrate Romance With One of Today's Hottest Authors

Amanda Scott

Experience the Romances of
Rosanne Bittner

More Zebra Regency Romances